SPIDERS

TOM HOYLE

MACMILLAN CHILDREN'S BOOKS

*This book is dedicated to the special few who
make me want to be a better man.*

First published 2014 by Macmillan Children's Books
an imprint of Pan Macmillan
20 New Wharf Road, London N1 9RR
Associated companies throughout the world
www.panmacmillan.com

ISBN 978-1-4472-5046-3

3 5 7 9 8 6 4 2

A CIP catalogue record for this book is available from
the British Library.

Printed and bound by CPI Group (UK) Ltd, Croydon, CR0 4YY

SPIDERS

Books by Tom Hoyle

CHAPTER 1

INTO THE WEB
(FRIDAY 31ST OCTOBER 2014)

'Let me out! Please, please, let me go. I'll do anything.' The girl thumped hard on the glass. 'Please!'

They wanted her to be happy, but they wouldn't let her go. She had to stay until they could all make the journey.

Thick darkness hung on either side of the dual carriageway. A lorry sped past, throwing up misty spray, its driver focused ahead, oblivious to the surroundings.

No one noticed a vehicle turning down the narrow road that snaked through empty fields. The car followed the road through a barren valley, then climbed up to where rocks replaced grass, before stopping by Loch Dreich, a cold and windswept place, one of the highest and most remote locations in the Scottish mountains. Trees bravely clung to the soil nearest to the lake, and here, where the road met the water's edge, the men left their car and took a track on foot.

One man carried a crowbar; another a hammer; the third, who was shorter and stockier than the others, had a large spanner along with six large plastic bags in his rucksack. Out of the night came the gentle lapping sound of water on rock. In the middle distance, perhaps half a mile away, they saw one glinting light and were drawn along the track towards it, like moths to a flame. Torchlight made pale circles in front of them as they strode closer through the misty moonless gloom. They were arrogant. Foolish.

Castle Dreich was an ideal target: isolated, grand, full of prizes. In this deserted valley, mobile phones did not receive: the residents would be helpless.

It would be easy . . .

Sneak: quietly approach, shrouded by darkness.

Crack: force the window open.

Thud: three thieves arrive next to the most valuable items.

The benefits of a prison education.

Greedy thoughts of rich jewellery and golden ornaments filled the men's minds. Farmhouses had been easy targets. This would be better.

Their torches shone across a web of tyre tracks, but there were no cars, and not a sound came from the large building.

'Look,' said the short, stocky one. He pointed at a

2

slightly open window and chuckled. 'Fan-bloody-tastic. Easier than ever.'

For a moment the half-moon shone on the loch, reflecting off its iron-like surface, and a smear of light ran up the hillside. But the three men were interested only in the window and the rewards beyond.

Unseen figures in cloaks, briefly illuminated by the moonlight, watched the men. One breathed in through glistening teeth and licked his lips. Then the deep black returned and those on the hillside were invisible again.

The castle was more or less square, traditional in its turrets and reddish-brown stone, medieval-looking apart from modern garage doors on the side facing away from the loch. Thirteen broad steps led up to a large oak door studded with metal. The men didn't know it – but the door was unlocked. To the right of it, along a narrow ledge, the open window tempted them closer.

Come in!

The men crept up the steps, rising above the lowest level of blank windows, and shuffled a few feet along the stone shelf to the opening. A quick flash of the torch revealed the treasure that lay inside. 'Let's do this,' said the tallest, nudging the window wider. Within seconds they were in an Aladdin's cave – a sitting room packed with valuables.

3

'Whoever lives here is going to get one hell of a surprise when they find this lot has gone.'

The shorter man leaned against the thick interior door, listened intently and then eased it open. He saw the inside of the front door and a wide central staircase. It had the faint air of a hotel lobby rather than the entrance hall of a private house. He crept to the next door on his right and opened it; his torch flashed across long dining tables until it reached a dumb waiter, there to bring up food from the kitchens below.

Back in the entrance hall, he could see a door at the far end that differed from the others – it was larger, older and not the same type of wood. Something made him edge down the hallway towards it. It was unlocked.

'Come on,' said one of the others in the first room. 'Let's get this done.' Items were smoothly swept into plastic bags from mantelpieces and tables: candlesticks, small twisted sculptures, dark paintings of mythical creatures.

Outside, figures surrounded the castle. They raised their hoods.

Inside, the shorter man opened the door at the end of the hall and peered into an old chapel that ran the entire length of the far side of the castle, bigger than most churches. Up and to his left, looking down on rows of

4

chairs, was a sort of viewing gallery. And to his right a table, with something lying on it. The man frowned.

Two torches darted around the first room, beams crossing, as the men moved faster and more greedily. Then one stopped: 'What the hell?' He was looking at a picture inside a gold frame. It was of a baby's body with a goat's head and horns. 'Weirdos.' His torch beam fell on to the next picture on the cabinet: it was of a dead pig.

At the far end of the room a music box started playing a simple tune, making them jump. They trained their torches on the box and the music stopped with a long screech. The two men froze.

'This isn't right. Where's Jay?' In unspoken agreement, they started towards the window they had entered by.

There was a gentle hissing sound above them. They instinctively shone their torches upward. Carved gargoyles leered down from the ceiling, words painted around them. The men read them aloud as each was illuminated: *Welcome to the Castle by the Loch.*

Then: 'Let's get outta here. Now!'

Suddenly the window snapped shut from the outside and a key turned in the lock of the door. For a moment there was light under the door, but then, bit by bit, it disappeared.

A peppery smell began to fill the room.

'Smash the window!' Neither one was sure who said it.

The crowbar was swung back, ready to come crashing against the glass and lead. But at that moment, melting out of the darkness, from behind the glass, came a face with wild eyes and an open mouth.

The smell was intoxicating – drugging the men.

Now the face at the window had horns.

The drug was taking effect.

Heads of snakes appeared from his ears, then slowly slithered out.

The man dropped his crowbar.

There was a voice: 'We will empty you of yourself.'

Shadows appeared to move inside the room. Their hazy edges became sharper as the shapes gathered into human form. They swirled round and round, faster and faster, distorted, twisted and ugly.

The tallest thief started to whimper as he saw that every figure had snakes' heads for eyes. The peppery-sweet smell in the room was overpowering. The man realized he was screaming. He sank to his knees as the faces came closer and closer until he was smothered by them.

Outside, someone laughed, the sound echoing off the hills and reaching out over the loch.

In the old chapel, the shorter man, Jay, edged towards the table. On the wall he could make out a painting of a large yellow circle with jagged spikes or rays firing out of it. Walking forward, he saw that a set of golden armour lay on the table. If he could carry this out, it would fetch a fortune.

Then he smelt something. Something sweet, even sickly, but also like pepper. Greed fought with uneasiness as the room started to swirl around him.

The armour twitched and spun. The hallucination had begun. Metal jolted and clanked.

'What the . . . ?' he slurred.

The helmet lifted off.

The visor was pulled up.

But there was no head inside – only bees gathering into a swarm. They were coming to get him.

The thin beam from the pencil torch made the patient's pupils constrict only very slightly. The doctor shouted to make himself heard over the screaming: 'Please sedate him.'

A needle was pressed into the man's arm, but he still struggled against the restraints that pinned him to the bed.

'Another dose.'

Eventually the man's struggling faded away into just the occasional twitch.

'Are the other two in the same state?'

Another doctor, holding piles of thick files against her chest, nodded. 'They seem to be terrified – we can't get them to speak or respond to more than basic stimuli.'

'The brain scans?'

She shook her head. 'Extraordinary. Very unusual brain activity. Some important regions of the brain are dormant, and others overactive. I don't think the frontal lobe will ever return to normal.'

The man on the bed roared and tried to shrink away from the serpents that coiled down from the ceiling towards him. His world was a blur of terrible images. Fear clung to him like clothes; his blood was thick with treacly dread.

The three men had been found earlier that day on Edinburgh's Royal Mile. One month before, on the night they lost their minds, these same men had arrived at the edge of Loch Dreich in the Highlands, intending to burgle a castle.

CHAPTER 2

NEW BOY
(FRIDAY 31ST OCTOBER 2014)

YEAR 10 AT GOSPEL OAK SENIOR SCHOOL, LONDON

'Incoming!'

The tennis ball bounced off the whiteboard. A good throw: via Megan's desk, it made it all the way to the back wall and nearly hit the poster about the Highlands of Scotland.

'Jake. Your go!' There was a murmur of excitement and some cheering. Jake had broken the clock and a fluorescent tube already this term.

Jake Taylor had grown in all directions in recent months and now shaved daily. He pointed at a boy with plastic-framed glasses sitting near the front: 'Leo, keep an eye out for Fanny.' Leo trudged forward, reluctant to do Jake's bidding but frightened to show actual opposition. Miss Frances was always late, especially when she had Year 10 for geography. As Leo peered through the glass panel in the middle of the door, Jake drew back his arm and let the ball fly.

It was one of those throws so strong and direct that the

ball didn't rotate in the air, right until the point where it hit Asa in the ear.

'Ooooh! Sorry. I didn't mean that,' said Jake, clearly as the introduction to an insult. 'I meant to hit your boyfriend.'

Adam, who was still waiting for his growth spurt, stood up and faced Jake as he had so many times before. 'You're *such* a knob.'

'Please, *please* don't hurt me,' mocked Jake. 'Please don't throw me out the window, special one.'

As so often, Adam's mind was dragged back to the events of the previous Christmas, captured by a cult, then fighting at the top of a London skyscraper, sending a man falling to his death . . . the police investigation that followed, and the attention – most of it unwelcome – that he faced at school. True, he enjoyed the admiration of the younger boys and the flattering attention of girls of all ages, but this was scant compensation for the lack of a normal life. He would have given up all of the flattery to just be normal. Worst of all, teachers were keen to be sympathetic to him and Megan.

Someone had passed the ball back to Jake. 'Let me have another go . . .'

There was frantic waving from the door and Leo scurried back to his desk. 'Fanny's coming.' This would usually have resulted in a leisurely and partial return to order. 'With Sterling.'

There was an urgent return to an unnatural standard of behaviour. Miss Frances walked in followed by Mr Sterling, the deputy head, who mumbled, 'I thought I heard a bit of noise. Must have been upstairs.' He turned to the doorway. 'Come in, Oliver.'

Oliver was blond and good-looking in the way that appealed to mums rather than to girls. He had large blue eyes and a round pale face. Adam's mum would have called him *sweet*. He carried a brown leather satchel – not the usual rucksack – and a strangely shaped case that Adam feared contained a violin.

'This is Oliver Arkwright,' said Mr Sterling. 'His parents have recently returned from Hong Kong. Oliver is a keen musician.' Mr Sterling paused and looked at the boy as if he was an unusual specimen under a microscope. 'I am sure you will fit in well, Oliver.' Everyone could tell that this remark was more in hope than expectation. A boy like this would have to adapt *very* quickly to Gospel Oak.

'Thank you very much, sir,' said Oliver in a high-pitched whisper.

'Why don't you sit next to . . .' Mr Sterling scanned the room, but the only spare seat was on Jake

Taylor's table. 'Er – how about . . . ?'

Adam held his breath and tried to look away, but Megan was keen to catch Mr Sterling's eye. She was even nodding slightly, indicating their table.

'Megan!' hissed Adam.

'Yes, why don't you join Megan and Adam over there? I'm sure they can squeeze one more on.' Mr Sterling smiled faintly at Miss Frances and left the room.

Immediately there was a rush of noise.

'Are you going to show us your big instrument?' said Jake.

There was the usual sniggering from the back, but the silence that followed caught Adam's question: 'What sort of music do you like?'

'The usual,' said Oliver politely. 'Bach mainly.'

The room fell about laughing, even Adam's friend Leo, who was relieved that a wonderful gift – an even greater geek than him – had arrived.

Megan *tried* to help. 'I'm sure you like modern stuff as well.'

'Yeah – Megadeth and Slayer,' shouted Jake.

Oliver might have been quiet, but he didn't lack nerve. 'Actually, I do like some of the heavy sounds.'

Thank God, thought Adam.

Oliver continued: 'Yes, I'm rather fond of the Beatles.'

CHAPTER 3

DOGS
(FRIDAY 31ST OCTOBER 2014)

Little warnings were all around Max.

Champion Swimmer Goes Missing shrieked the board next to the newspaper seller.

A boy was borrowing the book *Kidnapped*.

Special DVD offers by the door included *Taken 2*.

He came out of the library and plugged himself into his iPod.

Max was a chess champion and had been in the paper under the headline *New Scientist – The Best GCSE Physics Result in Britain*. He had a free place at the poshest school in the north of England.

He walked in time with the beat of his music.

Behind, a man and a woman walked in time with him, but with slightly longer paces. Step by step, they drew closer. At the corner they waited to cross, all three together, closer than was natural. It was instinct that made Max pull the cords from his ears.

I'm safe here, he thought. *This is my area. And there are lots of cars.*

It was then he felt a tiny sharp pain on the back of his neck, like one single hair being pulled. But when he put his hand up there was nothing there. He glanced at the woman; she gave a fake smile, showing her teeth, but her eyes were blank, like a dog's.

The man put the thin needle back in his coat pocket.

Max walked on, but despite speeding up and slowing down, he couldn't get more than a couple of paces away from them. His wariness developed into fear and then something more like terror. He imagined sharp teeth set in protruding jaws.

He heard a yelp. *Stupid imagination*, he thought. Then, in the distance, he heard a howl.

When he came to the path after the bridge the people were no longer there, but his fear remained; it was like the fear that makes you check behind the sofa and under the bed after watching a horror film, the fear that makes people want to sleep with the light on. Every little sound was a threat.

Don't be stupid! Why can't you think properly?

The instant he put the music back on he was surrounded. Shadowy, vague shapes appeared. He could hear growling, then barking, getting sharper and louder.

Dogs. His worst fear.

His eyes were blurred and he couldn't blink them away. Yelping and howling, ever closer. The shapes became more like people, but not quite *people* . . . they were hunched over, with bent legs and arms.

Max could see their hair – dogs' hair. Their faces: DOGS' HEADS.

What's happening to me? I'm going mad.

They were around him, jostling, barking furiously – slobbering against his face – making his heart race. Terror bolted through him like lightning. He tried to shout for help but it emerged as a strangled gasp.

They were inside his head, the noise echoing in his brain. He tore at his own face. He barked and howled like a wolf. He put his paw to his face and felt bristly fur.

He bit his hand and shook his head from side to side, trying to shake his arm from his body.

Max fell to the ground.

When he woke up, he was 260 miles away.

Max wasn't the only one. Eleven other children were taken in the second half of that year.

Champion Swimmer Goes Missing.

Brilliant Young Musician Disappears.

School Maths Genius Vanishes Without Trace.

Other papers carried similar stories. An artist, a computer designer, a linguist (seven languages) and a writer all disappeared without a trace. All were aged between fourteen and sixteen. All were considered prodigies – the best of their generation.

They were taken by people willing to wait for the ideal opportunity to take the right person. It was important that no talent was missing.

When Max awoke, he could see eleven other captives. But there was one place remaining. A central place. A *thirteenth* place.

Those who had taken Max had a very strong belief about who must fill it. Someone who had already proved himself unique.

'Let me out! Please, please, let me go. I'll do anything.' Max hammered on the glass. 'Please!'

They wanted him to be happy, but they wouldn't let him go. He had to stay until they could all make the journey.

CHAPTER 4

OLIVER
(FRIDAY 31ST OCTOBER 2014)

At lunchtime, Asa sidled alongside Adam, his face knotted with worry. 'Adam, mate, I have a crisis.' Asa was often having crises. Three-quarters were girl-related, and most of the rest were to do with clothes.

'Yeah? Has Rachel discovered the size and shape of what's in your pants?'

'No, she hasn't.' All sorts of thoughts were bubbling up in Asa's head. 'Well, maybe she has.'

'Ah. That *is* a crisis.'

Asa looked Adam right in the eye. 'Biology. After lunch. Mrs Cook. Homework. Not done. Me no comprendo. You're my only hope.'

'No way!' said Adam through his teeth. 'You're not copying mine.'

'Adam, man, you're my saviour. And you copied my history last week.'

'I got a detention for that, you idiot. I'm telling you, you're not copying mine. No. Can. Do.' He put his hands up in a double-stop signal. 'Look: mine's a copy of Meg's with a few mistakes thrown in to make it look genuine, which I got as long as I didn't let you anywhere near it.'

'That girl wears the trousers in your relationship.' Asa's face had the cheeky look that usually preceded something rude, but another thought soon occurred to him. 'In that case, I'll have to copy Leo's. Greedy bastard. Come on – I'll have to get to the shop: his price has gone up – it's a Dairy Milk *and* a Galaxy. You'd think I'd get a reduction as his best customer.'

Going out of the school grounds was strictly forbidden for anyone below Year 12, but Adam and Asa had made the journey a handful of times, despite the warnings and threats (and alleged dangers) associated with such an expedition. As they headed across the playground, Megan and Oliver walked towards them.

'Hi, Meg,' said Adam. 'We're just going for a walk.'

She immediately looked suspicious.

'Yeah,' Asa added, 'just off for a bit of fresh air.'

Megan was about to do her best to stop what was obviously a trip to the shop, when Oliver mentioned that he would like to join them on their walk.

'You'll be fine with us,' said Adam, pleased to take Oliver with them. 'Nothing can go wrong.'

'Look after him,' Megan said, smiling.

'OK, Mum,' said Asa, who kept talking as they wandered across the playground. 'Oliver, you're gonna have your first lesson into the dark side of Gospel Oak.'

Adam took over, his arm on Oliver's shoulder. 'Oliver, let us show you the three S's.' They went down some steps and passed what used to be bike sheds. A few boys and girls with black hair and pale skin were hanging around. '*Skivers*. If you want to bunk off a lesson, this is the best place to come.'

The trio were met with blank stares and silence.

After the disused weather station they passed a tatty brick-built bungalow. 'The old caretaker's house,' said Asa. On the far side were two entangled couples. '*Snoggers*.'

One of the girls opened her eyes and saw the passing trio. 'Hi, Asa, Adam,' she said in a brief pause. One of the boys waved.

Ahead there was a narrow opening in a line of bushes and a bit of worn grass that indicated a track. Inside there was a sheltered area about eight feet square. Boys and girls from Years 12 and 13 sat on logs. '*Smokers*,' said Adam.

'Adam, dude,' said one of the boys.

Then they dashed into the shop, which was right next to the track's exit. 'You break my heart,' said Asa as he saw Adam buying some liquorice, obviously for Megan.

Oliver had been quiet for most of the journey, but now he spoke up as he looked out of the window. 'That blue Toyota was in the school car park earlier. Same number plate. And I saw the driver in assembly.' The car was reversing into a space opposite.

'You're right,' said Adam, exchanging impressed nods with Asa. 'It's Mr Baxter out to buy a packet of fags.'

They paid very quickly – the shopkeeper keen to assist regular customers – and ran.

Adam and Asa handed in their work to Mrs Cook. 'Thank you,' she said. 'This looks good.' The boys were very pleased with themselves.

Infectious diseases had started off as a topic with lots of potential, but most of the class had long since lost interest filling in worksheets and copying from the board. Adam and Asa had somehow evaded the seating plan and were together on the back row, behind Megan and Rachel.

'Great scenery,' said Asa, just loud enough to be overheard, as Rachel bent over to get something from her bag.

The lesson – a double – had reached that happy point, about halfway through the second period, when Adam and Asa realized that the interest of the few, and the general misbehaviour of the many, made it possible to get their phones out.

'Candy time,' said Asa as he started playing his latest obsession. Upright textbook as a shield, Adam was risking Angry Birds Star Wars when he heard Oliver.

'The majority of infections start as asymptomatic,' Oliver was saying. Megan and Leo seemed to understand what this strange language meant. 'And the book isn't right about Japanese encephalitis. It comes from pigs more often than birds.'

'Ha!' said Adam, leaning over to Asa. 'That'll put a sock in Leo's gob. Oliver knows it all.' He glanced at Asa's phone; now he certainly wasn't playing *a game* – there was an image of a very attractive woman wearing not very much. 'LDR?' he asked.

'Yep.' Asa was admiring a picture of Lana Del Rey. 'Fit. And look at this.'

Oliver's detailed explanations of diseases receded into background noise. This time it wasn't Lana Del Rey. It was a blonde girl on a beach, topless.

'Great tits!' said Asa.

Adam nodded and grinned in enthusiastic agreement.

Somewhere in the distance, Oliver again corrected Leo on a point of detail.

21

Then—

'I'll take that.' It was Mrs Cook, plucking the phone, image still on display, from Asa's hand. Megan and Rachel flanked her as she peered at the screen. 'You two are disgusting. You're coming to Mr Sterling's office right now.'

Adam could feel his face redden as Megan looked up from the picture and shook her head, lips tighter than usual. 'But – it – we –' he stammered.

'They suddenly popped out,' mumbled Asa, searching for the right words to plead with Mrs Cook. 'I mean popped up. I mean . . .'

Phone first, held at arm's length like a dangerous specimen, Mrs Cook marched the boys to Mr Sterling's office. She outlined the course of events with worrying accuracy.

Mr Sterling waited until Mrs Cook had left the room. He didn't know how to make the picture disappear from the screen so put it face down on his desk. He asked all the usual questions that didn't really have answers. 'Why were you not concentrating?' and 'Don't you want to learn?' and 'Are you unaware that phones are banned in lessons?'

Adam and Asa answered everything with apologies.

'And what lesson was this in?' he asked.

'Sorry,' said Asa.

'Biology,' said Adam.

Mr Sterling glanced at the picture as he handed the phone back. 'Evidently.'

CHAPTER 5

ABBIE
(PAST AND PRESENT)

'You can't cross without paying respect to us, and that means money. Now.' He held out his palm.

The wasteland was easily the fastest route home from the centre of town. 'Yeah? And you three psychos are going to make me, are you?' Abbie Hopkins sneered. Her blue eyes, narrowed and fierce, glared from boy to boy.

The middle boy, holding a stick, was emboldened by having his mates on either side of him. 'Pay now. Or else . . .' He tapped the stick in his palm.

It was a stupid territorial matter. No one was allowed to pass through this wasteland without giving respect to the gang leader. The boys were fourteen- or fifteen-year-olds playing at being gangsters.

'Just show *respect*,' said the scrawniest of the three in a voice that was not quite broken. 'This is our land.' He kept glancing at his mates.

'Or maybe we'll make you give us something else . . .' Now it was the tallest one on the right, who really fancied himself. His square jaw and broad shoulders meant that

24

he was the only one with any hint of menace. He looked at Abbie's tight grey T-shirt and shoulder-length blonde hair.

Their victim snarled. 'I'll give you my knee in your balls so hard they'll pop out your eyes.'

Victim? Abbie stood with her head on one side, showing no fear at all: a stand-off with three boys on one side and one girl on the other. *Fair odds*, she thought.

She tried going left, but was blocked, so shoved the boy backwards with both hands. He caught one foot against a piece of metal and sprawled on to some bricks. He looked up at his mates, silently urging them to do something.

Without warning, the stick came towards Abbie, catching her on the chin. Instinctively her hand went up to the wound, returning covered in blood.

Before she could react, all three boys ran, fast. From a safe distance away, they whooped and gestured rudely.

'Come back here . . . Come on! I'll take you on all at the same time!' Abbie hurled a series of insults at them as blood ran off her chin and dripped on to weeds.

That was how she got her scar. She was thirteen at the time.

The next three years had not been easy for Abbie. Her father's work took him away from home for long periods, and it was during one of these times that her mother became sick, going from slender to skinny, and then becoming pale and weak. It was after two months that the doctors used the term *cancer*, but that word was never said again. 'Six months to a year to live' actually turned out to mean a scraping-down-a-blackboard decline over about two years until finally life was wrenched from her.

At the funeral, Abbie was surprised by how little she knew of her parents' friends – and how little she knew about her dad.

Abbie thought it was stupid having a party after the funeral. She spent a while shrugging off embarrassing adults simpering the same unhelpful drivel, then went up to her room and listened to 'One' by Metallica over and over again until everyone left.

'Abbie, come down,' called her father. 'We need to talk.'

Half-eaten pork pies, cake wrappers and other detritus of the party were left scattered around. 'Yeah?' said Abbie, turning up the depressing music her dad was playing.

Her dad pressed stop. 'Now is the time for us to think about the future.'

She looked at her dad. He was virtually a stranger. 'OK.'

'I'm into something at work and want to see it through. It'll mean some time away. Maybe a month or so. You

can stay with Uncle Brian and Aunt Anne. You like them.'
Uncle Brian and Aunt Anne were the type who still went
to Ibiza in their fifties.

'Sure.' Abbie wondered what was going on behind
her dad's heavy-lidded eyes. 'OK.' She turned and went
towards the photo albums that were lying on the table.
These were the old pictures – the ones that weren't on the
iPad. The front page had a photo that had been taken
at school when her parents were not even Abbie's age.
Everyone else was looking at the camera, but her mother
and father, arms around each other's shoulders, were only
smiling at one another.

'Did you ever have any girlfriends other than Mum?'
Abbie asked.

'No.' The word sounded like *Of course not*.

Abbie flicked through the pages. Uniform turned to
casual clothes, school to university, and then to their first
small house – but the two of them were always together.
Finally, pictures began to include Abbie: the three of them
very close, on beaches, in amusement parks, on a hilltop.

Things had been different before the illness came.

Abbie wasn't just trying to say the right thing; she
meant it when she said, 'We'll never forget Mum, even
though she's dead now.'

Her father flinched, then frowned. 'Dead?'

'Yes. She's gone. She died!'

'No. You're wrong,' her dad muttered, turning away. 'She's not dead. I think I know where she is.'

ONE MONTH LATER

The sitting room was lit solely by small candles along the windowsill and running down the middle of the table between the two men.

A slim but imposing man turned over cards with strange runes drawn on them. 'She's thinking of the special place you went to on holiday.'

Abbie's father leaned forward. 'Isla Canela in Spain,' he muttered.

'Yes,' the man continued in a partial trance, his eyes shut for a few seconds. Another three cards were flipped over. 'There is interference, but your wife is saying something about water.'

Abbie's father laughed. He remembered the pool, the sea, the water park.

'She says that there is water where she is, on the "Golden Planet". Lakes and rivers.' He paused and ran his thumb down his cheek, then turned another card. 'She says that there are only a few other people there.' His hands went flat on the table, white at the tips as they pressed hard.

The only sound was the faint dancing of the candles until Abbie's father whispered, 'Is there anything else?'

'Yes,' the man replied. 'She says that she will love you, always. And that your daughter must not know of any of this yet.'

Yes, he thought. This is complicated enough. Abbie wouldn't understand.

CHAPTER 6

A GOOD SHOT
(SATURDAY 1ST NOVEMBER 2014)

Asa's birthday party was a small but friendly event. 'I thought about a huge house party for all the local girls,' he said to Adam and the others, 'but felt sorry for you saddos.' Oliver had been invited along after pressure from Megan to include the new boy.

They had been paintballing a few times before, but never to Alpha Force. All of the usual traditions were observed: it was a misty dull day, huge muddy puddles formed a moat around the check-in hut and the place was staffed by laid-back twenty-somethings. Rachel declined the breakfast of burger smothered in tomato ketchup, but all four boys and Megan wolfed them down. 'Do you have any muesli?' asked Rachel.

Megan found it awkward holding a gun again after the events of last year, but as the layers went on – collar and combat suit and waistcoat and gloves – it became an increasingly surreal experience.

Deep Darth Vader tones came from inside Adam's helmet: 'The force is with you, young Meg.'

Asa, in his black costume, was striking a ninja pose, waving his arms in front of Leo and Oliver. Then he put his hand on his heart and went down on one knee in front of Rachel: 'I am here to protect you.'

Rachel's gunslinger stance made it clear she felt that she didn't need protection.

The marshal explained that they would be playing against another small group, a six-a-side football team. Their opponents were sixteen and it looked like an unequal contest. The girls claimed not to care about the outcome, but Adam knew that they were as keen to win as he was. Asa was downbeat and thought the competition was a bad idea, especially when Naresh – captain of the football team, whose preparation involved changing his T-shirt, revealing a knot of muscles – said that good-looking girls were an advantage because they tended to be better shots.

The first game involved having to defend an old church. Adam rolled around in mud and threw himself across floors. He was being braver than the others realized: four large bats were drawn on the sides of the hardboard steeple, and even their cartoon features made him shudder a little. He hated bats. Megan was a very good shot, found an excellent vantage point and spent most of the game picking off the opposition as they left cover. The church was defended.

'Nice one,' said Asa.

Going on the attack in the second game wasn't as easy. Adam was hit in the neck, Leo was hit almost everywhere (including the most painful place of all), Rachel in the chest, and Asa returned entirely yellow, claiming that Naresh had kept on shooting unnecessarily. Only Oliver and Megan seemed unscathed.

They all sat together at lunch. Adam was full of excitement about the little triumphs of the morning, and he and Naresh were at the centre of one big conversation.

As the pizza was eaten and shared, Asa laughed because Rachel had been hit twice, making it look like she was wearing a bikini top. Asa's observations on the scene were interrupted by mild violence.

The last game of the afternoon, based around the capture of a London bus, was the most exciting. Everyone agreed this would be the decider.

Naresh was the VIP they had to capture or kill. He strolled off towards the bus, surrounded by his five friends, and Adam gathered his team together. 'Look – you pin them down from this side, and I'll run round and creep up on them from behind.'

Adam's first cover was a tree. He was unseen. Then, after running six paces, he dived behind a log. Lying flat, he peered over and saw the bus, its occupants distracted by the onslaught from the other side.

A few more steps and his back was against a wooden shield. It was working – he was much closer.

Then he was behind a telephone box, gasping with exertion and excitement.

A few seconds later, behind a London Underground sign, partially hidden and just a few feet from the bus.

Edging forward, gun rising, behind his opponents' backs . . .

Nearly there. Targets in sight.

He raised his gun and took aim.

'Don't even think about it, prisoner.' Adam slowly moved his head to the left. Naresh's gun was a few inches away.

'Bollocks.' Adam was marched into the bus, his arm holding the gun limp by his side, his mind racing about how his team could still win the game.

Naresh shouted over the sound of splattering paint: 'We have a prisoner!' Six guns pointed at Adam. 'We have a prisoner!' they chorused.

'Keep on firing!' shrieked Adam, loving the game, his

capture a source of frustration and excitement in equal measure, but his words were lost inside his helmet and covered by a flurry of pellets exploding against the bus.

Those in the bus returned fire, and Megan and Leo – and then Asa – were hit.

Suddenly there was a blur of movement and a figure vaulted in through one of the bus windows. Oliver's left hand was needed to make the jump, but his right fired a yellow splodge into the upper chest of one of the older boys and then into the stomach of the boy next to him. Oliver fell behind one of the seats, but his gun rose above it: one shot hit a boy over the heart, and the next two impacted into the backs of the fourth and fifth boys, who were rapidly trying to find cover at the front of the bus.

Naresh grabbed Adam, holding him in front as a shield, his gun on his neck at point-blank range.

Oliver stood up. Everyone was astonished at what had happened.

'Well done, Oliver! That's a draw. Let's call a truce,' said Adam.

Naresh saw Oliver's stare and hesitated for a second, still holding on to Adam. But being outdone by Oliver was a little too much for him to bear – so Naresh turned his gun on Adam again.

Then:

Phut!

Phut!

Two shots.

Naresh's world turned yellow. A shot from Oliver had hit him in the visor – otherwise it would have gone straight in his left eye. And as he put his left hand up to clear the egg-like mess, he saw that his right hand, the one holding his gun, had also been hit. 'OK, OK, game over,' he said, irritation creeping into his voice.

Adam was amazed that not a drip of yellow paint was on him. He turned to Naresh, who was still struggling with his soaked visor. 'Thanks, mate. That was great,' Adam said.

Naresh wanted to complain that the rules had been broken, but relaxed and slapped his hand down on Adam's helmet. 'Yeah, good one.' He glared at Oliver.

Oliver smiled and gave the tiniest of shrugs.

CHAPTER 7

ABBIE'S DISCOVERY
(SATURDAY 1ST NOVEMBER 2014)

History wasn't a strong subject for Abbie. And it made her angry about how people, usually *men*, behaved.

'Why don't you copy out that page?' her father had vaguely suggested without properly looking at the book. It was on Winston Churchill. He might have won the war, but he wasn't in favour of giving women the vote or India its independence. Pig.

'I need a pen!' But her father had gone out. She wasn't sure where – they both came and went without explanation. 'How can I do this without a pen?' she shouted at the front door.

She opened her father's study door. It was meant to be out of bounds. As she leaned across his desk Abbie saw a piece of A4 with strange shapes on it and a diagram showing phases of the moon. *What a mind-numbing job. No wonder he's distant.* Underneath, only half an inch showing, there was a photograph. Frowning, Abbie slid it out: at first she couldn't work it out, but then she realized it was of a bruised arm. And there were other pictures as well: a strange-looking castle next to a lake, a blurred photo of a man taken from a distance, a sheet of paper titled *Cult – Type B*, with the Metropolitan Police logo at the top.

At the top of the final sheet it said: *Undercover Placement into Low Risk Group.*

Abbie heard the front door close. She quickly pushed the papers back into their order and went back, without a pen.

Abbie's father was as vague as usual when, as they ate in front of the television that evening, Abbie steered the conversation around to what exactly he did. 'You know that I'm a police officer and investigate groups and gangs,' he said in a monotone. 'What makes you ask?'

'Nothing.' *Nothing* was often Abbie's response, so the conversation jolted into silence.

They finished at the same time as *The Simpsons*. 'I have to go out. I've some work to do,' her father said, taking his own plate to the kitchen.

Abbie wasn't sure where the impulse came from to follow her father that evening. She was meant to see some friends, but she wasn't in the mood. Boys were always hassling her, seeming to think that blonde hair and blue eyes and a short skirt meant she was an easy target. But she also had a desire to avoid copying out a timeline on the Nuremberg Trials.

It proved easy to follow her father into town, but she was astonished when he went to a taxi rank and sat in the back of a cab. They had their own car – a fairly new Mercedes. Unable to stop herself, she ran to the one behind and delivered the cliché: 'Follow that cab.'

Abbie was conscious that she only had £15 on her and watched the meter anxiously as they drove out of the town. Then her father's cab stopped outside an ordinary-looking detached house.

Abbie swore under her breath. It must be a girlfriend's house: her father was protecting her in the stupid way that adults think they should. She actually wanted him to get a new life; her mother wouldn't have wanted him to rot.

But why not use the car?

Abbie had never hidden behind anything in her life, but now she ducked behind a hedge.

'Hello, Mark.' Abbie could just about make out male voices, then a woman's voice and the distant clunk of a closing door.

Maybe this woman was a prostitute. That would be beyond sad.

As Abbie nosed out from behind the hedge, another couple went up the path. He was in a tie and she was dressed like an old-fashioned housewife.

She heard banging on the window to her right. An old woman was shooing her away as if she was a cat: 'Move on, whoever you are,' came through the glass. 'Clear off.'

Abbie mouthed back, 'Keep your hair on, you stupid cow.' She flicked up her middle finger.

She decided to walk past the house – just once. A quick look. It was getting dark and the light was on in the sitting room, so she would have a good view.

It didn't look like anything too weird, just a group of people sitting around a table chatting, but at exactly the wrong moment her father looked into the gloom outside, their eyes met and Abbie stopped walking.

Three people came to the window. Abbie waved. She could see her father say *my daughter* and some other words. The door opened and Abbie was beckoned in. He was saying, 'My daughter is so excited about everything I've told her.' And to Abbie: 'But when I said you couldn't come, I meant it.' He put his hand around her shoulder – the first time that that had happened in a long time. He hadn't even done it at the funeral. 'It's good to see you, Annie darling.'

Annie? Darling?

Abbie looked around the room.

The old-fashioned housewife spoke. 'Perhaps you will join your father in the Castle? Great work is going to be done there and in our secret London temple.'

'Er, yes,' said Abbie, with no idea what she was agreeing to. 'I suppose so.'

'Well, that's decided then.' This voice was lower. A man with a brooding sense of ownership over the proceedings came forward from the corner of the room. 'There's little time to waste. I'm sure that *everyone* will want you to come along.'

Back home, Abbie's father was angry. 'Even *you* must understand that there are some things kids shouldn't be involved in,' he seethed as he shook baked beans into a saucepan.

'I'm not a kid,' Abbie drawled in her usual way, letting her body sag.

Her father snorted.

Abbie was furious. 'I'm sixteen!'

'This is a more important job than you realize,' her father moaned. 'Now I have a serious problem: I'm expected to do a couple of months of residential work, and they think you're coming too. You've put the *entire* operation at risk. It was never part of the plan to take you along.' The beans were beginning to sizzle and burn.

Abbie understood that men like her father could be installed *undercover* into organizations possibly damaging to the state – religious fanatics, political extremists, environmental activists, anyone who looked dangerous. This group was suspicious because they had past links with troublemakers. His investigation was a secret to everyone outside a small unit in the Metropolitan Police and Thames House, the headquarters of the security services in London.

'I'll just come with you,' Abbie said with a shrug. 'It means we won't have to bother Uncle Brian and Aunt Anne. You said that this is just religious nuts in a big house in the middle of Scotland.'

Abbie's father explained again, very slowly, as if Abbie was five, that there would be no phones and no contact at all with the outside world, except through his coded messages, and that he had to retain his cover at all times – even when they were alone. Abbie would probably get very bored.

But Abbie thought it sounded like an adventure, something to liven up her dull life *at last*. Something to help her get over her mum's death. To get her away from this place where she was surrounded by memories.

Forty-eight hours later permission had come for Abbie to go undercover with her dad, but only because she was sixteen. She had to sign the Official Secrets Act, which meant that she would go to prison if she told anyone what her father was doing. It was *Annie* and *Dad*, a family involved in the group because they were searching for meaning in their lives after a recent bereavement. Cover stories, her dad explained, were always as near to the truth as possible.

'Minor stuff,' the man in a grey suit had said when she went in to sign the papers agreeing to keep everything a secret. 'It's a group funded by rich grannies and run by middle-aged oddballs. It's just a formality because of the past connections of some members of the group. Nothing can go wrong.'

Abbie had nodded at him and smiled.

'The most important thing is that you stay detached. Remember that it's work. Isn't that right, Mark?'

'Absolutely, yes,' said her father. 'We're just there to observe and report.'

*

42

That night Abbie's father returned to the man with the runes and received more messages from his dead wife. Mark Hopkins was excited about finding out more at Castle Dreich. This had become more than a job to him – the line between work and actual interest, even belief, was already getting blurred.

CHAPTER 8

THE VICTIM
(SATURDAY 1ST NOVEMBER 2014)

The evening after paintballing amounted to no more than pizza, crisps, cakes (all as usual) and a film. There had been considerable disagreement about which movie to watch: the boys wanted something violent or funny (preferably both, with zombies); the girls wanted a romcom, but would compromise depending on who the male lead was. The boys argued that good-looking actors always made bad films. So in the end they watched *Hot Fuzz* again.

Things went well until about halfway through the film. Adam was on the sofa with his arm around Megan. This was no longer done secretly: everyone knew that they were an item. Leo was on the far side of Megan, and Asa and Rachel were sitting on the floor in front of him, resting against one another, shoulder to shoulder, as if this was an accident of the seating arrangements.

Everyone agreed that Oliver was now fully part of their gang, especially after his exploits at the end of the paintballing. He was sitting with them, captivated by the film. 'I wonder if any of this actually happened,' he said, just as the front door bell rang, its chime going on longer than usual.

Asa leaped up but hesitated when the bell rang again – this time for even longer – and was accompanied by thumping on the glass and wood of the door.

'Better see who it is,' said Adam. 'Maybe your parents have forgotten something. I'll come with you,' he added, trying to reassure Asa.

It was clear that there were kids outside. Asa muttered about ten different swear words in succession as he took a deep breath and warily opened the door.

Jake stood on the doorstep. He burped aggressively in Adam's face. 'We've come to join the party,' he slurred, spurred on by his three grinning mates. 'If it's on Facebook it must be for everyone.'

'Just go away, Jake,' said Adam. 'You're not wanted here.'

'What are you going to do?' he said too loudly. 'Call the police? That hasn't helped you in the past.'

Megan arrived behind Adam's shoulder and Oliver also forced his way forward, apparently emboldened by his earlier heroics.

Jake, his breath strong with the smell of lager, looked down on Oliver. 'What's the pretty boy doing here? He's like that fish we looked at in biology – not boy or girl.' He turned to Megan. 'I really fancy you. Let's see your tits.'

Megan snarled.

Adam stepped forward. 'If you don't leave,' he said, searching for words that captured his anger, 'I'm going to mess you up.'

Jake made an act of speaking slowly and rather wearily to Adam, as if it was all too much trouble. 'You don't impress me. You don't impress anyone. You're nothing.'

Then an unexpected voice made everyone pause:

'You should leave now.'

Confident, balanced, accompanied by a step forward: it was Oliver.

At that moment Rachel came forward waving her mobile. 'I've called my parents and they're on their way over. If there's trouble they'll call the police.'

'Huh.' Jake shrugged and swore, looking at Oliver. Then, mimicking the Terminator: 'I'll be back.' And slowly, very slowly, he and his friends sauntered off.

The party reached an uneasy and slightly early conclusion: the spell that had hung over the day had been broken by the interruption. Oliver left first, and then Adam and Megan walked home together. It was a misty but mild night and they soon relaxed and started laughing about how birthday parties still consisted of paintballing and pizza and a movie. As their houses neared, Megan said, 'Maybe birthdays will never change. What have you got your mum for tomorrow?'

'Oh no! I completely forgot – and dad gave me a tenner for a card and chocolates.' He dug around in his pocket and pulled out a crumpled note. 'I'll have to run back to the twenty-four-hour shop. You go on.'

They kissed goodbye and then Adam ran off, calling, 'See you in the morning.'

When he turned the corner, he saw the body.

It was in the gutter behind a parked car. Adam spun around but there was no one to help. He edged closer, frightened, but aware that the person was in no state to harm him. He could see a pool of dark red glistening slightly under the street lights.

Then he noticed the familiar leather jacket, and as he pulled the body over, his hands now red with blood, he recognized the skull T-shirt.

Jake.

The body moaned. 'Make him stop.' He was alive.

As he tried to move Jake on to his side, Adam looked at the misshapen nose, bent to the right and pressed against his cheek, and the bright red bruises on the forehead. Smudges of blood soon covered Adam's clothes.

There was a cord tight around Jake's neck.

'Don't worry – I'll get this off you,' Adam said, compassion outweighing knowledge of who the victim was. 'You'll be fine.'

The cord had cut into Jake's skin, and there was more blood as Adam peeled it away. He stood up, cord in hand, as two men walked along the pavement towards them.

'What's going on?' said one.

'Please help,' said Adam. 'My friend has been hurt.'

When the police arrived slightly after the ambulance, Adam was still holding the cord.

I'm going to mess you up.

Everyone had heard him say it.

CHAPTER 9

HARMLESS? (DAYS FOLLOWING WEDNESDAY 5TH NOVEMBER 2014)

Abbie pulled her door shut and wandered down to the old chapel where there was going to be a talk. Her father had saved her a place. She thought of all the things she'd like to say to him. This had been a bad idea after all.

This was her third talk. There seemed to be little connection between them, but she assumed everyone else understood a lot more of them than she did. The first one was all about symbols, some of which were a bit disturbing, such as ugly faces with twisted horns, but others were just random squiggles. The most important shape was a circle speckled with gold and with jagged lines coming out of it. This, the presenter said, represented the 'Golden Planet' – the place where all 'Loyal Servants' would be taken one day. Abbie drifted off a bit in the middle. *Nutters*, she thought. *These people are mental.*

The second talk was about openness in the group. Abbie felt uneasy and actually did listen to most of it. Apparently there should be no secrets in the group, and nothing should remain hidden. 'We are naked before one another,' said a woman. As everyone had their clothes on, Abbie hoped this was a figure of speech.

Today's talk was about the 'Golden Planet' and how it was going to be ruled by thirteen exceptional people, led by the 'chosen one'. There was something about these people not knowing at first that they were special. Complete madness. Abbie began to glaze over again. Someone had been watching too much *Doctor Who*. But she had to pretend to pay attention. Her dad was paid to keep an eye on these lunatics, and she had no choice but to play along, though she wanted to scream at them for being *so* stupid.

As they stood up to leave, another family came over. 'Hi, we're Robert and Andrea. This is Noah.' The boy, also about sixteen, looked shyly at Abbie.

'I'm Mark, and this is Annie.' There were smiles from all, even – just about – Abbie.

'I thought that was really interesting,' said Robert. 'We've been here a couple of weeks and I must say it's excellent to receive such nutritious teaching.'

Nutritious teaching? Abbie groaned inwardly at the phrases the group used. They had their own way of speaking that was almost as daft as their ideas.

Noah stared at Abbie, briefly forgetting his embarrassment.

'I find,' Robert continued, 'that the longer we stay here, the more we understand of this world and the need to escape.'

Abbie smiled and nodded the moment they looked at her. She wanted to escape too. But not quite in the way Robert intended.

The meeting ended and they went their separate ways. Abbie had a long walk back to her room, going through the main entrance hall, up the wide stairs, up another set of stairs on the right, then left down a long corridor with windows that overlooked Loch Dreich. At the end she had to go left again to reach her room. It was a maze. She dragged her feet, fed up.

Later Abbie went outside with her father and they sat, slightly apart, by the water.

'I think this is a really wonderful place,' he said. 'I like the bare rocky mountains. It reminds me of your mum.'

'Yeah. S'pose. How long do you think we're going to be here?' Abbie whispered.

'We may need to stay a little longer than I anticipated.' Her father looked distant. He had been spending a lot of time talking to others in the group, or reading the group's materials, or gazing into space.

Abbie was feeling a bit unsettled, but wanted to hide it. Confusion wasn't a feeling that she was familiar with. It must be because she was so bored. She thought she heard a noise behind her, but turning, saw no one there.

Again: a scuttling sound. Still she could see nothing.

Abbie's father looked ahead at the wind blowing ripples on the loch, and for a few seconds they seemed to make the face of his dead wife. *Another sign*, he thought.

Behind them, under swelling clouds that were about to deliver rain, stood Castle Dreich.

A few days later, Noah plucked up the courage to approach Abbie. 'Hi, Annie.'

Abbie had decided he was wet, but she tended to think all boys were either weak or unpleasant – or both.

'Hi, Noah.' She mustn't be rude or sarcastic. 'Have you met the other kids here?'

'No. Not really. I certainly haven't spoken to any of the chosen ones.'

Abbie didn't understand. She was about to ask what he meant when, out of the corner of her eye, she saw a spider scuttle across the floor. She caught sight of its long legs tapping erratically, making it veer unpredictably, approaching her – and then darting away. She held her breath and felt her skin buzz with fear. She hated being afraid of something so small.

'Annie?' said Noah, looking at her closely. 'Have you seen something?'

'No, it was just . . .' She could hardly say it – even the word made her insides cold. 'Just a spider.'

'Oh.' He didn't make fun of her.

Abbie couldn't shake off the uneasy feeling. 'What was that about some of the other kids?'

'I'm really not supposed to say,' Noah said awkwardly. 'Bolleskine knows that you're new.'

Without thinking, Abbie flipped into her usual impatient and aggressive tone: 'Noah – don't be stupid. What do you mean?'

Noah smiled uncomfortably as his parents came within earshot. 'Good to talk to you, Abbie. I've heard Bolleskine speak very highly of your father. He said that he's making rapid progress.'

Bolleskine was still a shadowy and aloof character to Abbie. He was always surrounded by people, subtly guiding the life of the castle, dispensing advice, moulding and inspiring people. He refused to be called *Leader* – in fact, he refused any title at all. He was just Bolleskine. Abbie wasn't even sure if that was his first name or surname.

When she first saw him in the castle, he said only one thing: 'Less of yourself, young Annie. Empty yourself so that you can journey with us.'

Abbie had thought it was a ridiculous thing to be told, especially in such a patronizing way, with his hand on her head. He was like a creepy uncle. But her father had simply smiled approvingly.

It was Abbie's rebellious nature, multiplied by boredom, which made her intrigued by the locked doors. She was being told YOU MAY NOT ENTER. *You may not . . .* these were tempting words. And there were lots of locked doors in the castle, which was much larger than she had first realized.

Abbie's room had a view of the loch and was on the side of the castle away from the front door. But she had no idea what lay elsewhere in the building. She had heard mention of the tower, the roof and the cavern. At unpredictable times of the night, she could just about hear cars coming and going, and the rotors of a helicopter, but she had never seen anything.

Then one time she saw that the large door at the end of the corridor on her floor was open.

Abbie had had a nightmare. She had never had one in

her life before she arrived at Castle Dreich. It was about spiders – in this case one huge spider. Its legs drilled into the bed on either side of her and its thorax drooped down towards her chest. Abbie swung her head from side to side and flailed her arms against the mattress, then kicked out, sending bed sheets across the room. The spider chuckled, its raspberry-red eyes full of malice.

The nightmare lingered into the time when she thought she was awake. Then the spider shattered like glass.

Abbie lay on her bed and panted, wiping sweat away. *Spiders are becoming an obsession – get over it*, she told herself. *There are bound to be spiders out here in the middle of the countryside.*

She padded to the bathroom that she shared with a couple of other single women. On her way back she didn't go into her room but was drawn towards the locked doors. Perhaps she had heard movement.

Just before the stairs that took her down to the main staircase she saw a door on the right that was ajar. Abbie pushed at it with one curious finger.

The first thing she noticed was that the colour was different: dark red walls rather than mild yellows. The lighting was poor. About three paces in on her right was a mirror; and another a little further on. Then steps going up.

She could hear someone shouting, but it was far away. Abbie stopped and strained to hear, peering into the gloom up the stairs.

'I'll do anything to make them go away. I don't want to see them any more.' It could have been Noah's voice.

'Abbie?'

She turned around and saw Bolleskine. He was very close. 'Yes?' she said. 'I couldn't sleep.' She folded her arms in front of her pyjamas – out of embarrassment? For protection?

He didn't ask for an explanation. 'Don't be shy or nervous. We have *nothing* to hide here. You and I have hardly spoken. But I hope that will change. The future is exciting, and I want you and your father to be part of it.'

Abbie felt some of her certainty return. 'I'm going back to bed now.'

He didn't move out of her way. He wasn't *exactly* blocking her, but he made no attempt to move.

There was more shouting in the background. Frantic and distressed, but difficult to decipher.

It sounded a bit like: 'Get them away from me! Get them away!'

Pushing past Bolleskine, she said curtly, 'Thank you.' Abbie was not going to be intimidated.

Bolleskine chuckled. The same sound as the spider.

Back in her room, Abbie looked at the lock on her door. If only she had the key. She put her back against the chest of drawers and forced about six inches of it in front of the door.

It was then that she thought back to what Bolleskine had said. He had said *Abbie*, hadn't he? Maybe she was mistaken. He must have said *Annie*. Yes, *Annie*.

Eventually she fell into an uneasy sleep.

The next day, Abbie's father was given permission to log into a website operated by a national newspaper. Using the name *thenewsman*, he posted a comment on an article about banking:

> There is nothing that can be done now to stop this sort of greed, except to report wrongdoing and hope that the authorities will use all their power to fine or imprison the guilty.

He read over the submission. It was awkwardly worded, but would sit easily alongside the other criticisms of the banking system. Counting across the page, his finger fell on the third word, then the ninth, the seventeenth, twenty-sixth, and thirtieth.

> There is **nothing** that can be done now **to** stop this sort of greed, except to **report** wrongdoing and hope that the authorities will use **all** their power to **fine** or imprison the guilty.

Nothing to report. All fine. Tomorrow the website and arrangement for his coded report would be different.

Her father's door was open, so Abbie walked in and looked at him over the top of the computer. She spoke in a whisper: 'Dad, I don't like what's going on here. There's a strange feeling that I can't shake off, like I'm being watched. Sometimes I think I see things, but then when I look, there's nothing there.'

Her father tapped away on the computer, Loch Dreich large in the window behind him.

She continued. 'What is going on underneath us? In the *cavern*?' She shivered a bit. 'It's weird.'

Mark Hopkins kept typing. 'And what else do you think?'

'I don't like Bolleskine. He looks at me in a creepy way. He's *gross*.'

More typing. Faster.

'I'm a bit worried.' Abbie's voice was much softer than usual. 'Dad, are you listening? I think you should warn those people in London.'

He didn't stop typing. 'Do you? Is that what you think?'

Abbie moved closer to her dad. 'I hear things and have bad dreams. It never happened to me before. I can't work it out.'

'I find it very difficult to concentrate when you're in here.' He glanced at his daughter as she leaned over the top of his keyboard. He focused on his screen, making her appear blurred, and finished writing his line:

. . . *of myself.*

Every line said the same thing, over and over.

I must become empty of myself. I must become empty of myself.

'Trust me,' he said. 'I know what I'm doing.'

CHAPTER 10

THE SNOW PLACE
(SUNDAY 2ND NOVEMBER 2014)

'I don't like Jake Taylor. In fact I really don't like him. But I didn't do anything to hurt him.'

Adam looked at the policeman, then at his parents, who nodded in agreement.

'I don't like Adam Grant. In fact I hate the little turd. But it wasn't him. I was confused at the time, like I said, but there's no way it was Grant,' said Jake.

'Well done,' his parents said.

'But in any case, Grant shouldn't go around threatening people. He should be locked up.'

Jake's parents stared at the policeman and nodded in agreement.

Adam sat round the kitchen table with his parents, the debris of a cooked breakfast scattered around them. They had exhausted the subject of Jake's attack (and rescue), and it had exhausted them. A glance between his mum and dad signalled an attempt to end the conversation on a happy note.

'Adam, darling,' said his mum, 'it's been quite a year, so we've booked up the usual trip to Bulgaria and have decided that you can go on the school trip as well. We thought you'd like to know before you go to the Snow Place.'

Skiing was the one proper luxury in the Grant household. Borovets in Bulgaria wasn't a glamorous resort, but they went every year and Adam had become a good skier. To also get a place on the school trip to Aviemore was the answer to desperate prayers.

The words spilt out of Adam: 'That's sick! Cool. Amazing. I can't believe it.' He hugged his parents in a way that teenagers rarely do. 'Can I tell Megan and the others?'

His fingers whirled over the touch screen on his phone.

Mr Grant shared in Adam's excitement: 'You'll love Scotland. It's a place you'll remember for the rest of your life.'

The Snow Place was an indoor ski slope on the outskirts of London. The others had decided to get in some practice there before the Scotland trip, so it was ideal that Adam was now going too. Oliver had been keen to join them when he'd heard them talking about it, so was going to meet them there. The journey, as Adam expected and feared, was full of talk about Jake. Adam's dad drove, saying nothing, though his eyebrows fell and rose as he listened to the conversation.

'I'm not surprised someone smashed his face in,' said Asa.

Adam was uneasy. A year ago he *had* been guilty of accusations levelled against him, though it was more complicated than that. He couldn't help thinking of the knife and the gun and the fire and the explosion . . .

'Adam? Adam!' It was Megan, keen to say something, *anything*, to bring him back. 'Which option shall we go for in Scotland?' They had to choose one other activity in addition to skiing, which they all took for granted. 'How about winter hiking?'

'I'm going to do skating,' said Rachel.

'Snowballing for me!' came Asa's voice from the very back of the Volvo.

'I don't know, Meg,' said Adam. 'I'll do whatever you're doing.'

The Snow Place wasn't large, but it was the biggest in the area: nearly 200 yards of 'real' (if man-made) snow with two tow ropes dragging skiers to the top.

Adam leaned on his poles at the bottom as Oliver and Leo slid alongside him rather awkwardly. 'Good luck, guys,' Adam said, and pushed himself towards the bottom of the lift.

Then, immediately and unexpectedly –

'Watch it, mate,' shouted a boy in his late teens as he swept down off the slope, nearly colliding with Adam. He was wearing a baggy top and orange beanie. He added, over his shoulder, 'You can't cut me up like that. Prat!'

Adam made his way forward again, this time alongside Megan, who was obliviously trying to blow smoke rings with her breath in the cold.

Suddenly, and equally without warning, another skier in his late teens arrived and sent a shower of snow over them. Laughing to one another, the two older boys pushed in front and caught the tow rope back to the top.

Adam, a graceful and fearless skier, looked very much the part in his black salopettes and ski jacket. To the others, bumps and lumps of snow were obstacles to be avoided, but for Adam they didn't seem to exist. Only Rachel was anywhere near as good, but Adam could beat her to the bottom every time.

They all relaxed. Leo put his skis into a wide V-shape

and stayed as near to the edge as possible. Megan was trying to give him advice: 'Push down on your left leg; now your right.' But it didn't help. Oliver was learning incredibly quickly: he had serious natural ability, just as at paintballing. Asa, wearing a jacket that was pink rather than red, and making repeated use of the phrase *poetry in motion*, spent most of the time cheering Rachel on.

On the third run down, Adam – carving to his right – somehow managed to lock skis with the same boy who had shouted at him earlier. Insults were exchanged as they fought to disentangle themselves before they became wrapped around one another and crashed in a heap.

'You little prick,' said the older boy. 'You completely took me out.'

Adam was indignant as he pushed his boot back into the binding. 'You were going faster than me, so it's up to *you* to avoid *me*.'

The boy was pointing his pole at Adam. 'Somebody needs to teach you a lesson,' he said, poking Adam with the sharp end of it. 'You should get out of people's way.' Another poke, which caught Adam in the neck. Then he swore, calling Adam a word that was rarely used, even at school.

'Just leave me alone,' Adam shouted, snapping in

his other ski boot and skiing off.

Still vaguely worried by what had happened to Jake, Adam spent the next fifteen minutes avoiding the boy, then realized he had gone.

'Come on, let's get a drink,' said Megan, hoping that they would return for a happier burst of action before they had to leave.

As they put their shoes back on, Asa could be heard saying something from the toilet, which was just off the boot room.

'Keep searching and you'll find it,' said Adam, his old spirit returning, and getting an elbow in the ribs from Megan.

Asa continued in a high-pitched tone.

Megan shushed everyone. 'Speak up, Asa.'

'Come here; come here right now; all-of-you-come-here.' It was a breathless, frightened voice.

Leo, who had his shoes on, wandered into the toilet. Then his voice could be heard too. 'Help! Come here now. And get help!' Leo didn't joke.

Adam leaped up and took a few quick strides in their direction. As he entered he could see part of a lifeless face and a bloody hand poking out from under the cubicle. 'Meg, get help!'

Megan ran.

Adam started to force the toilet door: it wasn't locked, but the body obstructed it. He could push it just enough to peer round.

There seemed to have been a fight inside the cubicle. The toilet seat was broken and the top of the cistern was smashed on the floor. There were two crater-like depressions in the boy's head. But Adam's eye was drawn to the dreadful sight of a ski pole sticking out of his neck. It looked as if it had gone a long way in – certainly far enough to be sticking upright. Adam looked away, but felt his eyes being drawn back to the pole and the boy's face.

It was the boy who had crashed into him.

Megan arrived with an attendant from the front desk and the other older boy. 'Is he in here?' the boy was saying, apparently unaware.

The other boy was slow to accept that his friend was actually dead, and it was only when several adults, one the first-aider, came from the slope that the children were forced out of the area. There was a horrible fifteen-minute wait before police and an ambulance arrived at almost exactly the same time.

In the Snow Place's entrance hall, Adam and Megan edged away to one side where they were hidden by a board advertising disco nights on the slope. 'I don't believe it, Meg,' said Adam, his eyes filling with water but short of actual tears. 'It's all happening again.'

'I can't . . .' started Megan. 'I can't stop seeing the . . .' She stopped again.

Adam put his palms over his eyes and breathed in and out deeply.

'It's so awful. That poor guy. Why do these things always happen around me?'

Megan steeled herself. 'It's all a dreadful coincidence. This time it *couldn't* have been you. You didn't leave the slope.'

'I hope everyone else understands that.'

They were both picturing the same awful image of the murdered boy.

CHAPTER 11

THE CEREMONY
(SATURDAY 15TH NOVEMBER 2014)

The noise of a helicopter woke Abbie from a dream about flying spiders. She was groggy and had no idea how long she had been asleep. After groping around for the light on the bedside table, she found her watch: it was only 11.18 p.m.

After ten restless minutes, Abbie opened her window and a whistling blast of icy air billowed into the room. She peered down three floors on to the frosty grass that was murkily lit for about twenty yards until the darkness gradually won. Invisible in the night, the loch lurked in the distance.

She heard chanting rising with the wind and could just about make out one section of what looked like a large circle of people looking into the clear night. Arms were raised and something was being said to the heavens, but Abbie couldn't quite make out what, even though the night was now silent. Stars and planets twinkled in the sharp Scottish sky.

Abbie dashed back and turned off the bedside light.

When she nervously looked down again, the circle had unravelled into a procession. She could just about see three people in the middle, dressed in white; they looked like Noah and his parents.

Why hadn't she been invited? In fact, thinking about it now, her father had even encouraged her to go to bed early.

Abbie shivered and was about to close the window when she noticed someone even more familiar. Her father. Behind him came other black-cloaked figures. One man's glasses caught the dim light: Alistair, a thin man, dog-like in his loyalty to Bolleskine, with a salamander-shaped birthmark on his cheek. And at the very back . . . She thought it was Bolleskine himself, but it was hard to tell.

Abbie sat on her bed but kept the light off, then went back to the window – now there was nothing to see apart from the frosty grass. She tried to lie down but was wide awake and restless. Over to the window again. Back to her bed.

'What the hell is going on in this place?' she muttered as she felt for her clothes in the darkness.

You're being bad, came a spidery voice. *Stay where you are. You'll be caught. You'll be punished.*

Abbie slapped her forehead and crept to her door. She

could certainly explain going as far as the bathroom. The corridor, unevenly lit by bulbs in old-fashioned glass fittings, was deserted. She tiptoed past strips of light under some bedroom doors, but most rooms were silent and dark. Almost everyone must be at the gathering.

Why hadn't her father mentioned it to her?

Soon Abbie was at the door that she had gone through the night before. She turned the handle slowly, quietly, and pressed gently with her palm. This time it was locked.

Turning around, her body tense, Abbie expected to see Bolleskine. But there was no one, just the erratic breezes that found their way into the castle. In the distance, she could hear low, regular chanting coming from below.

Abbie shivered as she paused against a stone wall. This part of the castle had kept a lot of the original features, but was comfortably decorated. 'This isn't a monastery,' she had heard someone say when they arrived, 'it's a house for us to live in *for a while.*'

Abbie reached the top of the main staircase and peered over the banister. Empty. She heard two sharp knocks, and then louder chanting. It certainly wasn't English. Latin? Possibly. German? Hungarian? It was all a mix of harsh g's and k's and then short flowing sounds that seemed to be entirely vowels.

Abbie dashed across the top of the staircase towards a large door opposite. This was one of the YOU MAY NOT ENTER places, and had always been locked before, but was now ajar. If anyone found her beyond that door, she wouldn't be able to talk her way out of it easily.

As before, the watery yellow on the walls gave way to dark reds. Every three or four paces there was a mirror. The chanting became clearer still. The procession must have come inside and entered the Great Hall, which was the name always given to the very large old chapel.

Suddenly Abbie heard a rustle of movement behind her. This was a straight corridor leading, presumably, to the balcony above the Great Hall – no alcoves or turns, though there were closed doors down the left-hand side. She tried the first. Locked. The second – also locked. She ran on down the corridor, unsure of where she was heading and fearing she would run, literally, into trouble. Ahead there was a small outside window and the corridor turned ninety degrees to the right. She darted round the corner just as a cloaked figure reached the top of the main stairs and went through the door that was still ajar.

Abbie didn't like sneaking around. As soon as she was round the corner, she made up her mind that if anyone gave her trouble on her way back they would regret it. *Bring it on.*

Then she heard the first scream. It wasn't a yell of pain – it was a screech of terror. Another scream, this time lower in tone, a man's voice, and then a third – 'No! Please no!' The three voices overlapped and mingled together into a chilling choir.

As Abbie edged from the corridor on to the balcony overlooking the dimly lit Great Hall, the screams became whimpers. Rising above them, she heard Bolleskine's voice. 'We welcome you as chosen ones who will travel to the Golden Planet.' Abbie slowly stepped forward. 'This is why we must escape this world,' Bolleskine was saying. 'This bread helps us to see the demons that surround us. Just as we know our guardian angels, the Valdhinians, are waiting for us on the Golden Planet, so on this earth there are demons to torment and mislead us.'

Abbie crouched down and crawled nearer to the balustrade at the edge of the balcony, from where she was now able to see the backs of cloaked heads arranged in neat rows. Lying flat on the floor, she peered through the wooden struts and saw Noah and his family in white cloaks at the front. 'Welcome to our family.' Bolleskine was addressing Noah. Then he turned to the congregation:

'We have new travellers to accompany us. We are now less than two moons away from our departure. Then we will be free of all the evil of this world. But we must become free of ourselves.'

Everyone chanted: 'We must become free of ourselves.'

Abbie saw Alistair step forward and whisper to Bolleskine, who nodded. Bolleskine first spoke in the same strange language she had heard earlier, and then seemed to translate his own words. 'A message from the Golden Planet for Laura: Michael says that the pains in your leg will disappear when you arrive . . .'

A woman gasped and said, 'Thank you!'

Abbie wriggled back from the balustrade as another couple of messages were 'translated'.

'. . . and, finally, a message for Mark.'

Abbie froze.

'Soon it will be just how it was when we were first married. Please come, with our daughter.'

Abbie dropped flat and lay still as Bolleskine paused. Her head swam with possibilities and fears. Her father had said this was 'a straightforward placement'. He must know what he was doing.

'Now approach for our drink from the chalice,' Bolleskine said.

Abbie had to see this. She moved closer to the edge.

Alistair, narrow-shouldered and gaunt, stood in front of Bolleskine and drank from a golden chalice.

Bolleskine said, 'Receive this drink from our angelic masters!'

As another person went forward, Alistair staggered away on to the stage, his face full of peace and delight.

Her father was next. He gave a tiny glance behind – towards Abbie.

Immediately recoiling, she shot backwards, sprang to her feet and hurried back down the corridor. As she turned the corner, heading towards the main staircase, she heard Bolleskine say, 'Remember that we are free! Free of all law! Empty of ourselves! Free!' There was cheering.

Abbie ran back up the stairs and along the passageway towards her room. She didn't notice the man standing in the shadows at the bottom of the main staircase, the man who had left the door ajar. The man who later told Bolleskine that Abbie had seen the ceremony.

CHAPTER 12

BATS
(SATURDAY 13TH DECEMBER 2014)

Despite having had weeks to get ready for the trip to Scotland, Adam was still throwing things into his case on the morning of departure.

'Right, have you got everything?' his mum asked as he bounced his case down the stairs.

'Yep.' He tapped different parts of his luggage as he spoke: 'New trainers, iPad, food for the journey . . .' He felt in his coat pocket. 'Phone.'

'I was thinking of underwear, shower gel, gloves, thermals and waterproofs,' his mum said before she hugged him. 'Have a great time.'

Three minibuses were going from Gospel Oak Senior. It wasn't an especially popular trip, but it did have a small and committed following, largely of Duke of Edinburgh Award types. Adam's friends had convinced their parents it was a good idea by claiming that it was useful for Geography GCSE.

Asa was waving goodbye to his parents' yellow Freelander when Adam and Megan arrived just before the seven-thirty deadline. 'Where's your case?' Megan asked.

'All the essentials are here,' Asa declared, pointing at a bag that was no bigger than aeroplane hand luggage. 'Lynx, razor and the finest collection of boxer shorts in the galaxy. I haven't bothered with things like pyjamas.'

'Razor?' mouthed Megan to Adam.

Leo's mum was fussing, asking about arrival times and handing over the contents of a sizeable medical cabinet to Mr Macleod, the geography teacher running the trip, and Miss Frances, his assistant. All dangers and diseases were prepared for, including those with no connection to the Scottish winter: '. . . insect repellent . . . hayfever tablets . . . Strepsils . . . and this is a very good homeopathic remedy for dry coughs – he gets those, you know . . .'

A tall, thin man in a black coat was speaking to Oliver about a hundred yards up the road. Adam had a feeling that the man was glancing at him, but he pushed the thought from his mind and loaded himself and his luggage on to the last of the minibuses. Inside, he could see Megan and Rachel greeting one another with excitement.

It was a lengthy journey to their overnight stay at Stirling, four hundred miles away, but the route was motorway throughout, so they managed the first quarter of the trip in just over two hours. Asa had tried to start up some rugby songs he knew from his dad, but Megan successfully tackled each attempt before they reached the second line. Apart from that, electronic devices kept everyone quiet, and there wasn't a hint of *Are we nearly there yet?*

Mr Macleod, excited by the return to his Scottish homeland, pulled into a service station and let his passengers loose with no more than a return time as guidance. The attack on Jake and the dreadful death at the indoor ski slope the previous month and subsequent murder investigation were temporarily forgotten, and the danger that lay ahead was unknown, so Adam lived in the happy moment.

While the girls were getting something to read on the journey, Asa discovered that the beans he had for breakfast were generating potent smells, sometimes accompanied by significant noises. At first he tried to blame Leo and/or Oliver, then claimed it was a passing jet, but after the usual exchange of 'He who smelt it dealt it' and 'He who said the rhyme did the crime', Asa owned up and referred to the odour as 'a fine vintage', and then as 'a new weapon for the army'.

He then told a joke that started with 'There were two nuns in a bath . . .' and Adam responded with one a

Year 13 had told him about something that he'd never dare mention in front of Meg.

Best of all for Adam, Megan dashed over and pulled him away by the hand. 'Look what I've seen,' she said. There was a magazine with the Triumph Daytona on the cover. Megan was baffled by Adam's interest in motorcycles – she knew nothing about them apart from what she couldn't avoid – but she saw how much Adam liked them. 'I'll get it for you.'

'Thanks, Meg,' said Adam, thrilled that she wanted him to be happy.

Then, rather than drifting into motorbike-speak, Adam spotted a face he vaguely recognized from Megan's wall on the front of a magazine: someone called Kendall Schmidt. 'Let me get this one for *you*,' he said.

Result.

Megan kissed him properly, in the middle of the newsagent's, ignoring a passing Miss Frances and a whooping Asa, who only stopped cheering when Rachel hit him on the head with a water bottle.

The journey continued as usual: games became increasingly dreary and most of the entertainment came from waving at people in other vehicles.

The final stop of the day was just a hundred miles from Stirling. 'Toilet only,' said Mr Macleod. 'No dithering around –' and then with a quick glance at Adam – 'or anything else.'

It was in these twenty minutes that Adam first started to feel strange. He didn't exactly feel ill, but there was something odd about his hearing, as if everything was hollow.

'You've probably eaten too many Haribos,' suggested Megan.

'I also had a couple of Oliver's cheese-and-pickle sandwiches,' he said by way of defence, but then imagined cheese and pickle and Haribos together in his stomach and started to feel a bit queasy as well.

'How about having an apple? They're good for you,' said Oliver, plucking one from his bag.

Adam couldn't explain what was wrong with him – it was easier for him to say what was *not* wrong. He didn't have a temperature, or feel dizzy, but he felt worried and unsettled. He didn't even want to mention it to Megan, but he felt *scared.*

'You certainly don't look right,' said Megan. 'Your eyes are really wide and staring.'

Adam thought:

Why are all these people looking at me?

Something else bad is going to happen.

Megan will start to hate me.

Leo said that he had something in his case that would help, and he plucked out three different medicines.

Adam's anxious feelings slowly evaporated, but he still felt strange when they arrived at the accommodation outside Stirling.

It certainly would have been a late night with plenty of messing around with Asa, but Adam thought he would take advantage of sharing a room with Oliver to get some rest. He curled up in the top bunk and pushed the thin duvet up over his ears.

He had lost all sense of time, but it was only thirty minutes later that he woke up, terrified. Adam didn't know the cause; he didn't even realize that he was behaving irrationally.

Where he should have seen the innocent lights of the smoke detector, he saw the demonic eyes of a hungry bat. The movement of the thin curtains became the threatening rustle of bats' wings.

And there was another noise. Someone crying out.

He could hear his own voice.

Pyjamas damp with the sweat of panic and fear, Adam fell down from his bunk and crawled to the door.

'Aaaa-dam.' Oliver's voice was low and from the back of his throat.

Adam spilt out into the corridor, shouting at he-knew-not-who and he-knew-not-what: 'Why are you after me?'

He stumbled past the other bedrooms, eyes glazed, panting. 'I need to get out of here!'

Rachel was whispering to Megan about Asa when they heard the noise. Megan leaped up and raced, barefoot and in her pyjamas, towards the sound. She knew that voice. As she opened the door, Asa appeared at the next doorway, pulling on a T-shirt.

Adam rounded the corner to the reception. Eyes. All staring at him. Mr Macleod, Miss Frances and the teachers from the other buses were standing with room keys in their hands.

Adam saw the adults leer and sway towards him, their features increasingly pinched and bat-like. 'Why is everyone after me?' Out of the corner of his eye he could see creatures hanging upside down from the ceiling – but when he looked they had gone. He had to escape.

As he backed away, Megan caught him. 'Adam, you've

had a bad dream,' she said, holding on to him from behind. 'It's me, Megan.'

Mr Macleod edged forward and forced a smile. 'Don't worry, Adam. You've woken up and are muddled, that's all.' They were used to being sympathetic after what Adam had suffered a year before.

Adam sat down on one of the reception chairs. 'Everyone is after me,' he said.

'No,' said Megan. 'That's all over now.'

'You're fine, you're fine,' soothed Mr Macleod, shaking Adam's knee gently, trying to reassure him.

Slowly, out of the haze, he began to understand that he was confused, began to realize that something was wrong with him – and that was the beginning of logic and recovery.

Megan smiled at him. 'It's just a nightmare.'

She was right. But the nightmare was just beginning.

CHAPTER 13

BOLLESKINE
(SATURDAY 13TH DECEMBER 2014)

Abbie was with her father in the main dining room of Castle Dreich. The communal lunch was drawing to a close and most people had already left. Bolleskine entered, lit by watery light from one of the small gothic windows. 'You asked to see me, Mark?' His voice was that of a doctor: confident and calm.

Abbie looked carefully at Bolleskine's face. Before now she had seen it only from a distance, or in shadow. He was probably about forty, but could have been anywhere between thirty and fifty-five. His face was mildly attractive for an older man – good-looking in the tanned and slim way that suggested an ex-sportsman. It was his eyes that were creepy: they were never still, as if he was searching for something – lizard's eyes, darting from place to place with intent. Those eyes looked over her again. Some of the boys at school examined her in a similar way, especially when she was forced to do sport. That was understandable – but this man was nearer her father's age, and that made her shudder.

Abbie's father hadn't answered, but he did stand up.

'Do step this way with me for a moment.' The voice expected to be obeyed.

Mark spoke with a half-smile. 'Yes, of course.'

As they were about to leave the room, Abbie saw Bolleskine turn and put a hand on her father's shoulder. The clatter of plates and cutlery stopped as Bolleskine spoke. 'Annie – you should come too. I think you should be part of this.'

Abbie tried to convince herself that this was the way her father had to operate. She understood that he had to immerse himself in the organization, become a trusted insider. She had been told that sometimes he would have to make sacrifices to discover bigger truths. This must all be part of his act.

The journey to Bolleskine's room took Abbie into a part of the castle she had never seen before. Similar-looking staircases led them up and down. Then they came to a long corridor with seven large paintings hung on the wall. Abbie paused and looked at the first one, which showed one soldier attacking another with a sword. According to a small label underneath, it was called *The Rage of Achilles*. The second was *The Worship of Mammon*. Abbie wasn't sure what that meant, but didn't like the image.

'Do you like our reminders?' asked Bolleskine, pointing as he spoke. 'The seven deadly sins: anger, greed, laziness, lust, envy, gluttony – and pride.' The last frame held nothing but a large mirror. 'Do come into my study.'

Abbie would never have entered Bolleskine's room unless her father had nudged her from behind. There were bookcases, a desk and chairs set out in the usual fashion, and there was a door leading on to a large balcony. But any normality was lost because of one extraordinary thing.

Mirrors. Everywhere. Image disappeared into image as the reflections bounced back and forth. Wherever she looked she could see herself. She was the centre of the room.

Bolleskine was relaxed, as always, apparently unaware of her astonishment and fear. 'The mirrors remind us that we must be empty of ourselves – to see ourselves from the outside. To be observers.' He sat at his desk. 'Do sit down.'

'Annie, you sit.' It was her father's voice.

'Mr Hopkins,' Bolleskine said to Abbie's father, 'do you have something to say?'

Abbie's father closed the door. 'I am here to tell you that I am working on behalf of Her Majesty's Government.'

'I know,' said Bolleskine. 'I know about the messages, and I know about your concealed weapon.'

Abbie's father – Mark Hopkins of MI5 – nodded, unzipped the lining of his jacket and pulled out a small handgun.

Abbie was stunned into open-mouthed silence.

Bolleskine seemed amused, light-hearted. He didn't seem concerned by the gun. 'There are many, many spirits here. I know that you have seen them.' He turned to Abbie. 'Perhaps you have begun to sense their presence as well.'

Thank God this will all be over soon, thought Abbie. *Let's nail this lunatic.*

Abbie's father approached Bolleskine slowly, gun in his hand.

Come on, Dad: get him right now. Arrest him!

Then he laid his gun on the desk. 'I wish to obey you, serve the spirits and make the journey to the Golden Planet.'

'What?' Abbie was unsure if this was part of the act. 'Dad?'

'Kneel down,' said Bolleskine, as he picked up the gun.

To Abbie's amazement, her father did. Should she speak? Should she grab the gun? But she had to trust her dad. She didn't want to mess up an intricate plan.

Bolleskine pointed the gun at her father's head. 'What if I were to pull this trigger right now?'

The room was spinning around Abbie. Reflection piled upon reflection into layers of confusion. Then a germ of a thought: maybe there were blanks in the gun.

There was an ear-splitting bang and Abbie winced. The gun was definitely loaded. The bullet had hit one of the mirrors and cracks ran off in all directions like a spider's web.

The gun was again pointed at Abbie's father's head, this time at point-blank range. 'You want to join me, but what if it meant death right *now*?'

Her father's gaze was unwavering. 'Then I would accept it. I know what I have seen.'

Bolleskine smiled. 'Good. I must have your total loyalty.'

'You have it. Mine and Abbie's.' He used her real name.

'And what if it meant your daughter's death?' Bolleskine stood up and pointed the gun straight at Abbie's head.

Dad, please.

Bolleskine continued. 'I know that she's not yet one of us.'

The gun, reflected a hundred times, was the only focus in Abbie's world.

Her dad didn't flinch as he said, 'I will accept it. I know what I have seen. We must become empty of ourselves.'

CHAPTER 14

DOWNHILL RACER (SUNDAY 14TH AND MONDAY 15TH DECEMBER 2014)

The next day began with no mention that anything embarrassing had happened the previous evening.

'Morning, Adam, all OK?' was Mr Macleod's only greeting, cheerier and slightly higher-pitched than normal, but not betraying much concern. Everyone had put Adam's odd behaviour down to the stress of the last year.

Sunday was spent in Stirling, mainly in the castle. The usual banter swirled around him, but Adam couldn't join in.

Usually he would have been the centre point of the action, holding all the different characters together, but today he felt fragile.

Eventually, in a quiet moment, Megan managed to ask Adam what was wrong.

'I do feel a lot better,' he said, 'but I'm really worried that something bad is going to happen.' He couldn't explain it without being specific, which was embarrassing. He bit his lip, but the words slipped out: 'I'm sure that some of these people are looking at me.'

A young couple passed and made eye contact with Adam. 'See?' he whispered. 'Why is it always me?'

Megan shrugged and tried to make light of it all.

As the day went on, and the poison slipped from his body with each breath, Adam felt more at ease. By the time they arrived at Aviemore he was at the back of the bus with everyone's attention on him, back to normal. 'And then, just when I was completely naked, Leo's mum came into the bathroom,' he was saying, 'so I was lucky there was a shower curtain to hide behind.'

'Thank God it wasn't my mum,' said Asa.

Everyone laughed – Asa's mum was unshockable.

'But then I could hear *her* about to undress.'

There were groans of horror from all – apart from Leo, who was silent and red with embarrassment.

'So I had to, er, reveal myself.' Hoots of amusement. 'And say that I was lost.' General spluttering at the ludicrous explanation. 'There were items to shield myself with. Fortunately.'

'Toothbrush?' suggested Asa.

'A *large* bottle of bubble bath, as it happens.'

Mr Macleod's voice came from the front. 'That's enough! There are ladies present.'

Asa made a great play of looking around and apparently seeing no one that fitted that description.

Mr Macleod again: 'And here we are. Aviemore! Cases off, please, and early to bed.'

The minibus door was rolled back to reveal thick and falling snow. Adam clenched both fists in celebration. 'This means that the slopes will actually be open. Mr Macleod, will we be allowed to go on the real slopes rather than the dry ones?'

He gave the sort of answer that teachers do. 'We'll see – if you get an early night.'

Adam was allowed to share with Asa. There was no repeat of the previous night, and Adam went straight to sleep and slept through till morning.

Aviemore was windier and damper than the resort Adam knew in Bulgaria, but the breakfast was an enormous fry-up, everyone was friendly, young and cool, and a PistenBully had already groomed the fresh snow on the slope by the time they arrived.

Rachel was unrecognizable inside her ski gear, encased in five layers and two balaclavas – even her hair was tucked inside for protection. 'Is anyone in there?' Asa asked, tapping gently on her ski helmet.

Adam had a rather more relaxed attitude to how much protection was needed, especially in the absence of his mum. Megan had frowned when Adam claimed four layers to Mr Macleod. 'Skin counts as one,' he had whispered.

The thermometer said minus five, but it felt even colder despite sunshine at the top, and some grainy snow was being blown around.

Their instructor was a young woman, tanned and relaxed, in a black and blue ski-school outfit. 'Follow after me,' she said.

Adam enjoyed being a better skier than the others: he leaned into a handful of turns, his body at forty-five degrees, then pointed his skis downhill: the wind rushed in his ears, the cold nipped at his exposed chin and he loved it. Then he dug in hard with the side of his skis when he stopped, spraying snow on to a board that displayed a piste map. 'Wow. Yeah!'

By the end of the morning they had done every run more than once. At lunch, the ski party sat together, sharing sausages and chips, while Rachel picked at a salad. In between challenges and boasts and mouthfuls of food, Adam gradually became aware of a group of four people sitting at a table across the room. He had the terrible sensation, again, that they were looking at him. *Don't be so stupid*, he thought. *You're over that.* But the more he fought it, the more his paranoia grew.

One of them was talking behind his hand, occasionally glancing at Adam.

'I think we should get back on the slopes,' Adam said, but the others weren't keen: it had clouded over and a mist had descended.

Adam left, going outside to put his skis on. 'Come on,' he urged as the rest of his group emerged from the mountain restaurant.

'Wait there, Adam,' said the instructor.

But Adam was sliding away already.

Halfway down the slope, he paused and looked back. Visibility was now poor, but gradually Adam saw . . .

One . . .

Two . . .

Three . . .

And finally four figures swept out of the cloud and headed straight towards him. They were the group from the other table.

One of them stopped in front of him, blocking his way, and within seconds the other three arrived alongside.

'We're here to collect you,' said the first man. A

birthmark on his left cheek ran from the edge of his goggles to the collar of his ski jacket. He was determined to follow Bolleskine's orders.

The woman was reaching in her pocket for something. Adam was transfixed. It looked like a pen.

'In time you will understand that this is the right thing,' the other woman was saying. 'You will see that you are very important.'

Adam saw that the pen was a syringe and took off a second before the needle swept through empty air. This time he made no turns at all. Fear kept him upright over bumps and he disappeared into the mist. He tucked his ski poles under his armpits and leaned forward, legs rattling up and down erratically. A skier swore as Adam cut him up.

Then the ski lift took shape in front of him – a tow lift like the one at the Snow Place. Adam scrambled forward on his skis to get on as quickly as possible. He had to make it back to the top and find his friends.

'They're after me!' he shouted at the man at the bottom, who waved and smiled back, recognizing Adam from earlier.

As he was pulled away by the lift, he looked behind and saw the adults appear. They were about five or six places behind him on the lift. The bad weather had deterred most other skiers, so there was no one to call out to, but Adam did have his mobile. Biting off his right glove, he pulled the phone from his pocket. It was wet with condensation, but – *thank God* – there was power and reception.

All the time the top of the lift was edging closer. Instead of calling the police or his parents, he called Megan. 'Hello, Meg,' he shouted. 'Help!'

'Ad—' she crackled intermittently, 'I – you . . .' The line bleeped. No signal.

Large flakes of snow had begun to fall.

When Adam was about five yards from the top of the lift, it stopped. Delays sometimes happened when someone had trouble getting on or off, and normally they went unnoticed. But now Adam shouted up the slope, 'Come on!' Turning to look behind him, he saw that the first of the adults had unclipped his skis and was hulking up the slope.

Perhaps Adam should do the same and try to reach the restaurant. It would be slow going carrying his skis though, and if the lift started up, he wouldn't be able to use it . . .

He couldn't ski down – that would be *towards* the danger . . .

Adam looked to his right. There was a cord stretching the length of the lift, occasionally carrying a red no-entry warning sign. Adam tried to remember what was on the far side. Going off-piste could be very dangerous, especially in poor visibility, and Adam couldn't see more than a few paces ahead now.

The lift still didn't move – the man was rapidly getting closer . . .

Adam unhooked himself from the lift and skied off to his right, the cord scraping his lip as he slipped underneath it. For five or six seconds he was ploughing through snow that reached up to his knees, going deeper into encircling whiteness. Then the snow dropped away from under him, and as his legs searched for solid ground, he felt himself falling.

CHAPTER 15

SPIDERS
(MONDAY 15TH DECEMBER 2014)

Bolleskine wandered into the kitchen of Castle Dreich. Personal property didn't exist in the commune; everyone slept in the same type of bed, washed in shared facilities and ate the same food.

The kitchen was clean and orderly, though industrial in scale, with the blistering ovens usually found in hotels or schools. Basic, wholesome food was in preparation as Bolleskine tapped what looked like a powdered spice into his hand. He spoke to a woman who held a large wooden spoon: 'We must teach Abbie discipline. Let's increase her medication slightly.' He turned his hand over and the yellow powder sprinkled into the lunchtime soup. Drugs. More of the peppery dust was added, measured in, stirred around. The same substance was dissolved into a cup of water.

'Good,' Bolleskine said. 'We must let the medicine do its work.' He turned to a short man with a pale, narrow face. 'I want you to order much, much more of this. A hundred times more. No – a thousand! Plans have been revealed to me.'

The man frowned. He had seen the consequences of getting the dosage wrong, as had Bolleskine. Those who consumed it quickly, especially by breathing it in, and in large enough quantities, had suffered horribly. Some had even died.

Bolleskine did not turn around, but sensed doubt. 'Just do as I say,' he said.

Abbie sat deep in her chair, her insides shrinking, staring at the creature in front of her. It had the head of a spider: lidless black eyes peered out from a face covered in coarse bristles; a bulbous abdomen-like sack was attached to its back, hanging down like thick hair; the body shape was human, but the arms were a spider's legs. The lack of hands made Abbie shudder.

It made ticking sounds, but Abbie understood. *You must obey*, it said, sounding like an erratic and noisy clock. *You must empty yourself and obey*.

This was the worst one Abbie had seen. The visions had been getting more distinct and lifelike, less like shadows and more like *spiders*.

'I don't think you're real,' said Abbie. 'Talking spiders don't exist.' She was trying to convince herself.

The thing pulled one leg across the floor and Abbie

saw, poking out where there should have been a shoe, the tip of another hairy, bony spider leg.

You have been here for a month, the spider-creature said. *Now you must join us as your father has. You trust your father.*

Somewhere deep in Abbie's mind there was a bit of logic left that defied what was in front of her. 'I don't believe in God or angels or anything,' she muttered, 'and I certainly don't believe in talking spiders.'

The spider's fangs clicked together.

'Go on,' she said, still pressing against the back of her chair. 'Say something that I don't know. Prove that you are not from my imagination. Tell me something.' She tried to stay calm but was struggling to find a simple test. Then an idea. 'Are there clouds in the sky now?'

The spider moved its head and its eyes flickered slightly as it looked through the small window behind Abbie.

It had been clear earlier, but fine weather rarely lasted long in the Highlands, and at this time of the year the mountains prevented direct sunlight from hitting Castle Dreich. Abbie had no idea if the weather had changed. She reached behind herself, eyes closed – terrified that the creature would attack – and pulled the curtains shut with one hand. She couldn't allow herself to cheat.

'It's cloudy,' clicked the monstrous figure.

Abbie repeated the verdict. 'Cloudy.' She knew that it would be overcast. Cloud often rolled in after sunny starts. Maybe such things as demonic spider-figures did exist, and it was in this unusual place that they could be seen. Maybe her father was right. Maybe this group was made up of 'the most liberated and important people in the universe'.

She slipped out of the chair, keeping as far away from the creature as possible, and pulled back the curtains. The sun had gone behind one of the mountains, but there was no mistaking the deep blue of the clear sky.

The creature was wrong. She was hallucinating; the spider *was* a figment of her own imagination.

It was when Abbie sat down for dinner and saw Bolleskine watching the food arrive that she began to build a theory. *If I'm being drugged, it must be the water*, she thought, *or maybe the food.*

'Come on, Abbie,' said her father, nudging the bowl. 'Eat your dinner.'

'I'm not very hungry,' she said. 'My stomach is a bit unsettled.'

'Shame,' said her father in a level voice that reminded

Abbie of their old life. 'The food is good here.'

Avoiding the main course was much more difficult. Eating well and staying fit were considered obligations for members of the community. 'I'm really not hungry,' said Abbie. 'It's probably a girl thing.' That was usually enough to end a conversation with her father.

Bolleskine slithered in, slim features and bright brown eyes hinting at abundant energy. 'You should eat something,' he said. 'We've prepared this especially for you. Or at least have a drink.' Large jugs dotted the length of the table.

'No, thanks,' Abbie said, looking at the water, the first hints of thirst appearing, but thinking of using the taps later.

After supper she went with her father back to Bolleskine's mirrored room. She could see a reflection of the mirror behind them as she sat down. The room confused her, and the more she tried not to think about water, the thirstier she became.

'We have no secrets here,' said Bolleskine, 'just as we share everything else.' He looked intently at Abbie, then turned to her father.

'Abbie, I want you to know about our work here,' her father purred, his mannerisms and expressions increasingly echoing Bolleskine's. 'We are building an incredible kingdom.'

Abbie nodded impassively.

'The kingdom is a great one – full of outstanding people,' Bolleskine said. 'We have gathered together the most able of the current generation to build our new world. It will be a paradise. A place where we overcome and embrace our fears, where everyone works together, men and women and children all equal, guided by an exceptional leader.'

'And that's you?' Abbie asked, unsmiling.

Bolleskine laughed. 'Ha! How you misunderstand me!' He shook his head. 'I am merely preparing the way.' He leaned forward, animated now. 'Let me tell you a story,' said Bolleskine. 'I was not alone in the early days here, but worked with a greedy, impatient man, who stole a third of our group. He was inspired and understood deep truths, but was a slave to his own desires. He was called Coron.'

Abbie thought she had heard that name somewhere before.

'Coron knew he would die if one chosen boy was not killed before the appointed time – and one second after this current year began, the prophecy was fulfilled,' Bolleskine continued. 'Coron was right. Despite his evil betrayal of

101

us, he was right about our leader: one chosen for us. And it is your father who will now go and bring him to us.'

'Who is this person?'

Bolleskine tapped a large leather book on his desk. 'His name is Adam. He does not know it yet, but he will lead us into the promised world.'

Abbie left in silence with her father. Her thirst had grown beyond a distraction and was edging into discomfort.

Toilets, sometimes in the same rooms as showers, were dotted around the castle as no rooms were en suite. Abbie mumbled that she was going into one as they got nearer to her room. She went straight to the nearest tap.

Nothing.

She turned the tap at the second sink.

No water there either.

The water supply to Abbie's part of the building had been cut off.

CHAPTER 16

OUT OF THE FRYING PAN, INTO THE FIRE
(MONDAY 15TH DECEMBER 2014)

Adam felt his stomach rise. Even in the midst of his chaos and fear, for an instant he thought of a rollercoaster ride. The first part of his fall took two seconds, during which he experienced a Thorpe Park sensation, and – immediately afterwards – understood that the fall would end with a dreadful crunch, probably on to rocks. He tensed and waited for it to happen, unable to hold in a yell.

Adam's skis hit the compacted snow and snapped free of their bindings; his boots dug against something hard and jolted him, making him groan as his lungs emptied. This saved his life: it deflected him away from a large and jagged rock and slowed his fall.

Three seconds after the fall began, snow hissed and then squeaked as Adam fell into a drift that lay against the rocks.

He opened his eyes and saw white all around, pressing against his eyes. It was the pain in his left shoulder that told him he was alive. He muttered to himself, 'I'm not dead.' Still lying on his left side, with his right hand he felt his chest and both legs, then patted his head and face. 'I'm not dead!'

He sat up and looked towards the sky. Snow was falling heavily and the mist was too thick for him to see more than a few feet in any direction. Pain seared through his left shoulder. Adam slid his right hand inside his jacket and felt the area. He had no idea how to tell if a bone was broken, but at least nothing was poking out.

High above, the four adults sent by Bolleskine realized that it was impossible to follow Adam over the edge. They peered into the billowing snow but could see and hear nothing. 'Let's ski down and then head up into that valley,' said one.

Shakily Adam stood. His left side hurt, his ribs in general, his shoulder in particular, and there was a bump on his forehead, but he had a short spike of excitement that he had survived such a fall. His mobile phone, though, was smashed to the point that green innards and dented silver circuitry were visible.

Adam saw that a greyness was mingling with the white. Dark came early this far north, and he would freeze if he didn't get down the mountain. One ski was pointing upright and undamaged as if he had stuck it in the snow for safe keeping and one ski pole (bent at a right angle) was still around his wrist, but the other ski and pole were nowhere to be seen.

Adam put on the one ski and started his way down the mountain, panting and wincing as he scraped over stones, but then it became a gentle slope and he made better progress. It was when the stones returned, and he was forced to remove the ski, swearing to himself about the obstacles, the falling snow and the overall wretchedness of his life, that he heard voices coming towards him.

'He just skied off, looking really stressed. We couldn't catch him.' Rachel was sitting in the middle of the group, shrugging her shoulders, confusion mingling with adrenalin.

Mr Macleod made frantic phone calls. Comments such as 'How could you just lose him?' and 'But it's such a small place!' didn't help. Then there was a quieter phone conversation, back turned, with Adam's parents.

Rachel was going over the story: 'Apparently he said to the guy who was at the bottom of the lift that there were people after him – but *we* were the only people after him.'

Megan bit her lip and looked at the swirling patterns on the carpet. Without a word she went over to Mr Macleod.

'Could I?' She gestured towards the phone.

'Mrs Grant, it's Megan. I'm so sorry about Adam. He really hasn't been right. He was convinced that people were after him. I'm sure he'll calm down and come back.'

As Megan gently convinced Adam's mum – gradually turning her anxiety into hope – she felt her own belief that Adam was 'just being a bit odd' ebb away. She knew that Adam was *not* mad. She thought of what had happened to Jake and at the indoor ski centre. Maybe she was losing her mind as well.

Mr Macleod spoke to all the group very firmly about the need to stay inside. They all agreed at the time, but later Megan realized that she had to disobey this instruction and leave.

Adam crouched down as the voices approached – there were two people, perhaps three. Risking a glance, he saw a bubble of torchlit mist coming towards him.

His listened carefully, desperately hoping that they were rescuers rather than pursuers. Then his eye fell on his remaining ski, poking out from behind a rock.

'. . . take him back to the castle . . .'

'. . . such an important mission . . .'

Adam screwed his face up and tried to force himself deeper down into the snow.

He lay absolutely still as the voices came level with him and held his breath when the snow around him was briefly illuminated. Then, agonizingly slowly – far slower than they arrived, it seemed – the voices drifted away.

Adam was suddenly conscious of how dark it was. The smothering white had now been replaced by a blanket of black. Adam found it impossible to go more than a few yards without stubbing a boot into a rock. He felt, rather than saw, the falling snow, which stuck to his face and forced its way into his mouth.

The cold began to wrap itself around him and bite through his sweat. Three layers, he knew, would not be enough to get him through the night, especially as there was nowhere to shelter. Adam had hopes of discovering a dry cave, ideally with the materials to start a fire – not that he knew what to do beyond rubbing sticks together – but these were open and treeless slopes.

Perhaps he should have handed himself over. It might have been better than freezing to death.

Abruptly and unexpectedly, Adam slipped and fell on his right side. After he heaved himself up, he swished his ski pole in frustration, only to find it thumped against something raised from the ground. Adam took off a glove and extended his hand into the darkness. Despite the deep thudding sound, he imagined touching a face or an animal . . .

It was a fence.

So Adam started going down, fence pole to fence pole, always downhill. The cold was inside him now and he felt a deep tiredness taking hold, but he didn't allow himself to stop – always downhill, trudging, sliding, plodding. He felt the ache in his shoulder, his hunger, his fatigue. *Anything would be better than this.*

A few minutes after he decided that he would have to sit down and close his eyes for a rest, he saw a glow ahead and the mist lifted slightly. It was the car park at the bottom of the slope.

'Adam? Adam Grant?'

He had been spotted stumbling out of the gloom. There were five vehicles in the car park: two menacing and empty 4x4s; a white Cairngorm Mountain Rescue Land Rover and two police Range Rovers.

A policeman ran forward and helped Adam the last few yards.

'I'm fine,' Adam said hoarsely and slowly. 'I'm OK. But stay with me.'

'You're safe now. We know who you are and we'll get you straight into Aviemore and check you over.'

Other people, hazy to Adam, were using walkie-talkies.

He was surrounded by police officers and burly mountain rescuers. He breathed a premature sigh of relief.

Mid-evening, Mr Macleod received the message that Adam had walked off the mountain, suffering from exhaustion and minor injuries, but otherwise unharmed. Adam was being taken to Aviemore Medical Practice to be looked at by a doctor, before possibly being taken to a hospital.

Megan had just gone to her own room when Mr Macleod knocked on the door and announced what had happened. 'Thank God,' he finished. He explained that he was going to see Adam but wouldn't be gone long. 'Miss Frances will be in charge,' he said, as he strode off down the corridor.

Rachel came over and put her arm around a tearful Megan as she sat next to her on her bed. About three minutes passed, during which a door opened and closed outside, unnoticed by the girls.

'I *wish* I could help him,' said Megan as she leaned into Rachel again. Then she leaped up. 'Maybe Mr Macleod will let me see him.' She dashed to the window to check that he hadn't yet set off. Mr Macleod and Oliver were talking together as they crossed the car park.

Megan opened the bedroom window as far as she could. 'Mr Macleod! Mr Macleod! Can I go with you to see Adam?'

'Megan, I *do* understand,' he said, reluctant to take her in case there was a scene, 'but Oliver has already offered.'

Megan then had one of those moments that changes everything: she felt fear and danger. She saw Oliver at the indoor ski slope putting his ski boots on. Putting his ski boots on! Near the end of the session. Before the dead boy was discovered. And he had left Adam's party early. Early! Before Jake was attacked. No one had thought of *Oliver*.

'No!' she shouted aggressively. 'I should go. Or Asa.'

'Megan –' Mr Macleod sighed (*This was exactly what I feared*, he thought) – 'we'll be back soon.'

'Stay there!' she bellowed.

But Mr Macleod and Oliver were into the minibus and away before Megan could put her shoes on. When she went back to the window there was only an oblong snowless patch where the bus had been.

Adam was sitting on the bed facing a doctor when Mr Macleod walked in with Oliver.

After greeting the teacher, Adam turned to Oliver,

disappointed that Megan hadn't come instead. 'Thanks for coming, Oliver. Very kind of you.'

'It's the least I could do,' said Oliver, hands in his pockets. In one, a mobile phone linking him to Adam's pursuers; in the other, a syringe containing the same powerful drug as had been fed to Abbie.

CHAPTER 17

WATER
(MONDAY 15TH DECEMBER 2014)

Abbie looked out on Loch Dreich, thirst reaching up from deep inside her, its sandy fingers scraping her throat and drying her tongue.

If only I had a mobile phone, she thought. *This lot could be put on trial for poisoning, if nothing else!*

Even her father? She had already lost her mother. Abbie punched her fist into her bed. *There isn't even a landline or a computer that I can get to.* One need stretched out in her mind, banishing all other thoughts: *I must get water!*

The loch here was small compared to Loch Lomond or Loch Ness, but it was larger than most reservoirs and lakes in England. And it was made entirely of fresh water from the surrounding mountains: millions of pints of drinkable liquid.

Desperation drove her on. If she could get outside, she could run thirty yards to the lake. Shoes and coat on, she pressed her ear to her door . . . All clear.

She slowly poked her head out. She could hear the

ticking of a clock and indistinct voices in the distance, but nothing near, and not a sound from her father's room.

She would have to go down two floors and somehow get out, where there was no security lighting, and then, at the end, pure, cool water . . .

Abbie could think of nothing but her thirst.

Planting her feet as quietly as possible, she followed the corridor around a sharp right turn and froze. Her father was standing in her way, a look of angry disappointment and fatigue on his face. He could have been waiting there, but it happened to be a chance meeting.

'Where are you going?' The words were suspicious, obstructive, hostile.

'I need to visit the bathroom.'

He took three steps back and pointed to the closest door on his right. 'Go ahead.'

'Thanks, Dad.'

He didn't respond.

Abbie went into a cubicle and locked the door behind her. The toilet itself was unflushed. She had a moment of excitement: the cistern! Water!

Empty. Someone had already used it and it hadn't refilled.

Abbie looked at the window above the cistern. As she

opened it, cold winter air rushed in and rattled the cubicle door slightly.

Outside, her father looked impatiently at the bathroom door.

Abbie saw Loch Dreich stretching out before her in the thin slither of moonlight, and the hard, wintry ground more than thirty feet below. She looked up to the two upper floors, and down to the ground, covered with thin windblown snow. The castle walls were smooth, built for defence, not for escape.

'Abbie? I want you to come out now.' Her father's voice was lower and flatter than it used to be.

Getting down was hopeless. Abbie looked at the old iron drainpipe running down from the roof and the one just below her that ran from the bathroom and joined it. *Ridiculous.* She was unsure that she could scramble down, even if the pipe could take her weight. Her feet would slip on the walls . . .

She could hear her father again.

A fearful madness – fear of Bolleskine, fear of *her own father* – and a desperate thirst-fuelled craziness pushed her on.

She stood on the cistern, then found herself crouching outside on the window ledge. Facing inwards she held on to the sill, edging down and dangling very briefly, until one foot and then the other found the metal pipe.

It held her weight. She edged along, the window gradually disappearing from reach, until she lunged for the main drainpipe.

Muscles rigid, hands aching with the effort, and three storeys above the ground, Abbie was now angled away from the window. She couldn't go back even if she tried.

Suddenly another fear hit: falling. She pressed herself against the building, her nose pushed hard against the stone, too terrified to move on, unable to retreat.

'Abbie?' Her father's face appeared at the window, that new look of determined fervour in his eyes. He looked at her and then down. 'Wait here. Don't let go of that pipe.'

She wasn't going to.

He disappeared for several minutes. Abbie felt that she didn't have the strength to hold on much longer, or the resolve to let herself fall. She tried to spread her weight and hold herself up as much as possible. Snowflakes fluttered in front of her eyes, spinning in the wind.

'Trust me.' Her father again. 'I'm going to swing this across so that you can hold on.'

On the third attempt, Abbie caught the rope and managed to twist it around her wrist into a crude knot.

'Now let go with your other hand.'

Abbie could feel that the rope was firm. She let go and grabbed the rope with both cold, rigid hands. Next she had to drop her feet away from the pipe and let her father take her weight. *I must do this*, she thought.

Finally she slid from the pipe and swung down across the castle wall to a point immediately below the bathroom window. Crenellated battlements loomed over her. But here there was nothing at all to grab on to. She was held only by her father and her own determination to cling on.

She was winched down, each little descent jolting her arms, weakening her grip on the rope.

'I love you, Dad,' whimpered Abbie, and pictured herself running for freedom after drinking from the loch.

'I love truth,' came her father's reply.

After a further short drop, Abbie reached the bottom of the wall. She looked up but couldn't see her father – he must have been there: the rope was disappearing upward, writhing angrily as it rose.

The loch lapped peacefully at stones about thirty yards away. She scooped up a handful of the fresh snow and put it to her lips. Instant, partial, relief.

Many windows looked out this way, but most were unlit as Abbie scurried towards the loch. At the edge, she scooped up water greedily, the cold making her gasp. With her hands cupped together, she collected handful after handful, ignoring the icy drips dibbling off her chin. Then she paused. She could hear footsteps and a cough. Someone sniffed.

Suddenly there were a large number of people outside, spilling around both sides of the castle. They were not in cloaks this time, but were dressed in outdoor winter clothes. Engines rumbled in the distance.

One man stood out ahead of the crowd. 'Did you think that your father would hand you to anyone but me?' Bolleskine shook his head slowly and mockingly.

Abbie looked for her father – and spotted him, a few paces away.

Bolleskine came forward and grabbed the scruff of her neck. 'You see how perfectly things are working together – how clearly the spirits guided your father?'

Abbie looked at the loch waiting to embrace her.

'You came out here wanting to drink.' He pushed her nearer to the water. 'Let me help you drink.'

He forced Abbie face down into the water. At first she was most aware of the bitter cold, but then the feeling of needing a breath rose. It started in her upper chest and got more and more urgent.

No one was going to help her, she realized. Not even her father.

Bolleskine pulled Abbie up and she drank in air, wilting towards the expanse of freezing water. 'Take her inside and ensure that she drinks well – with our water. And give her some solid food as well.' He turned to Abbie's father and two other people. 'We must collect Adam tonight. Take everyone from the Inner Guard apart from two for the caverns and two for the castle. I'm going to get Adam myself.'

If the intention had been to intimidate Abbie into submission, his actions had the opposite effect. With the resolve that comes to one who has been given another chance, she was determined to find out about the castle and the caverns that lay beneath.

CHAPTER 18

COMING TO GET YOU
(MONDAY 15TH DECEMBER 2014)

Megan ran into the hostel reception and asked where Adam was.

The receptionist looked at her blankly.

'Adam Grant,' Megan persisted. 'The boy who is injured! The boy Mr Macleod has gone to see!'

The woman was in no hurry to deal with rude kids. She raised her eyebrows dismissively. 'The Aviemore Medical Practice. Not far. On Muirton,' she said with her soft Scottish lilt, 'just off Grampian Road.'

Miss Frances had followed Megan down the stairs. 'Is something the matter?'

'Miss, I have to go. To Adam.' Megan was already heading towards the door, typing *Muirton, Aviemore* into Google Maps on her phone.

'No, *no*. You have to stay here, Megan.'

Megan opened the door.

'Megan!'

She stepped out and the door closed.

'Megan, don't be stupid! Come back here.'

119

Megan ran.

It was not far as the crow flies, but Megan could see that she had to weave through side streets to reach the medical centre. Tennis and hockey had made her a good athlete, and she was a half-decent cross-country runner when forced, but she'd set off at a sprint. The first few hundred yards were easy, but after that, even though she slowed down, she was struggling for breath and her thighs and calves hurt. As the centre neared, her legs felt like stinging balls of rock. She urged herself on, sucking in air desperately and ignoring the pain.

Ahead was the minibus, left at an angle in haste, looking abandoned rather than parked. Nestled behind it were three Toyota Land Cruisers. To the far side, in the actual car park, a very reassuring sight: a police Range Rover.

Megan slowed to a walk. It was a residential area and she had to look like an ordinary kid wandering home, so she slowly drifted away from the street lights and into the darkness under trees, casually glancing around, before she crouched behind a wall, pulled out her phone and dialled 999. Whispering, Megan asked for the police and then said that a boy was in danger. 'I can see a police car already there,' she told the operator as, to her great relief, two tough-looking policemen emerged from the centre. Megan was advised to speak to the officers.

Just as she was about to run towards the policemen, she heard her name: Megan James. *What?* She frowned – and stopped.

'Roger. If we see her, we'll bring her back. Over and out.' It was one of the policemen speaking into his radio. Miss Frances had wasted no time contacting the authorities.

Megan dropped down behind one of the Land Cruisers. From inside she could hear the dull rumble of conversation, one word of which made her stop breathing: 'Adam'. Then she heard it again: 'Adam', and – even worse, confirming her fears – the name 'Oliver'.

Crouching close to the ground, Megan headed towards some low bushes on her right that ran down the side of the single-storey medical centre. The ground was hard and slippery, laced with the knotty roots of trees and peppered with small shrubs. Looking to her left as much as she could, glancing between Land Cruisers and policemen, she held her breath for the twenty yards until she was down the side of the oblong building.

The first door that Megan came to was a fire escape – simple to open from the inside, but impossible for her on the outside. As she turned down the long rear side of the building, she realized that she couldn't get in: no open windows, no second entrance, nothing. Smashing a window would bring everyone running. The police would just grab *her*. Hopeless.

Dr Tomlinson turned to Mr Macleod and Oliver. 'I need to give Adam a check-over now, so you'd better wait outside.'

Adam liked Dr Tomlinson. Her manner was friendly, more like a nurse's than a doctor's. Adam was surprised at how young she was, and that her make-up and clothes suggested she was off for a night on the town.

She turned to Adam with a smile. 'I'll decide if we need an ambulance to take you to hospital once I've had a quick look.'

Adam smiled. Nearly a year ago, he had been in more ambulances and police cars than he cared to remember. His smile was more of relief than excitement: he felt much safer now that there were policemen nearby and Mr Macleod and Oliver had arrived.

'Why don't you slip your top off and I'll have a look at that shoulder?' Dr Tomlinson helped ease the T-shirt off Adam and then squeezed the area gently with her fingers. 'How does that feel?'

'Tender. But not too bad.'

There was further pressing of Adam's side. 'I don't think anything's broken. But we should keep you in overnight for observation. You can call your parents and let them know how you are.'

She then examined Adam's leg. Adam felt mildly embarrassed taking his salopettes off and sitting on the bed in bright red boxer shorts that were probably a year or so too small for him.

'Yes, you're in one piece, although that shoulder will be sore for a few days, I expect, and you won't be skiing any more this week.' Dr Tomlinson was taking her gloves off near the sink. 'I'll have a word with your teacher while you get dressed.' Adam had stayed on the bed to avoid parading his boxers in front of her, hands and arms obscuring as much as possible. She went out without turning round.

As soon as the door closed, Adam heard his name. Then again, and a series of taps on the window. He went over, unthinking, as he put his T-shirt on – and could see Megan's face, ghost-like, at the glass.

'Adam, open the window!'

As soon as he did, she hissed with desperate urgency, 'Get dressed and climb out. You're in danger!'

'But—'

'Don't waste time! I'll explain later.'

Adam clicked the lock on the door from green to red. Then he threw on his clothes, relieved that Mr Macleod had brought him trainers to replace his ski boots, and too flustered to think to hide his tight boxers in front of Megan.

Dr Tomlinson returned a few seconds after Adam had dropped down out of the window. 'Adam? Have you locked the door?' She rattled the handle. 'Adam, can you open it when you're changed?' She listened and could hear nothing. 'Adam?'

Mr Macleod had been talking to the policemen about Megan's disappearance, explaining that she was bound to turn up at any second, when he heard Dr Tomlinson's voice and rushed from the reception, Oliver following. Mr Macleod joined in, knocking, ordering, persuading, pleading and above all regretting the disaster that his trip had become. 'Adam? Adam, will you open this door?'

Not a sound.

'Can you open it?' Mr Macleod asked.

'Yes. There's a key that overrides the lock.' Dr Tomlinson ran off to another room.

Oliver's mind worked differently. Mr Macleod saw

Adam as a worried schoolboy barricading himself in a room, probably huddled in a corner; Oliver saw Adam as an anointed leader, though one unaware of his status. Oliver left the geography teacher and went to the front door.

'Oliver, come back!' shouted Mr Macleod. Now he had lost *three* of his group.

Oliver calmly went to the policemen standing outside the building. 'My teacher has asked me to tell you that Adam is locked in his room and won't open the door.' A half-truth from an angelic face. 'Could you go in and help, please?'

The policemen immediately went inside.

Oliver ran to the Toyota Land Cruisers. 'He's escaped – probably out the back. Inside are two police, one doctor, one teacher. Quick.'

Bolleskine instructed three of the people getting out of the first car: 'To the left.' Then, to three from the other car: 'Go round to the right.' He held his hand up for them to pause for a second. 'I need Adam tonight. Kill anyone who obstructs our glorious work.' As they left, he spoke to the man next to him, Abbie's father: 'Get the cars to sweep around over there –' he waved his hand imprecisely towards the residential area behind the clinic – 'but try to keep it low profile.'

Finally Bolleskine turned to Oliver. 'Well done – you will be greatly rewarded when we arrive at the Golden Planet.' He put his hand on Oliver's cheek. 'Your parents are proud of you. I have spoken to them twice in the past week. They are enjoying their stay in our new home.'

Oliver thought of his parents and remembered them drinking the liquid that enabled them to leave their bodies and be the first people to depart Castle Dreich and make the great journey. He knew it wouldn't be long before they were reunited.

Behind the Medical Centre, they fought their way over a frosty fence and then dropped down behind a low wall. 'Megan, what the hell is going on?' Adam hissed hoarsely.

'Maybe nothing, but I –' she put a finger to her lips as they went across a car park – 'I think something bad is happening again. We need to keep moving.'

In front of them was a large modern school that looked very secure, so they followed a path that curved to the left and came out in a residential street.

After turning a couple of corners, straight ahead they could see what looked like the main road. Suddenly headlights were coming from that direction. 'Watch it,' said Adam as he pushed Megan behind a large black dustbin.

A Toyota Land Cruiser slowly drove past.

Megan's head peered out around the side of the bin. 'That's them!'

Mr Macleod and two policemen watched as Dr Tomlinson unlocked the door. He had expected to have to cajole a frightened Adam out from under the bed, but dread beyond panic erupted inside him when he realized that the window was slightly ajar and the boy had gone.

One of the policemen opened the window wider and poked his head out. 'Adam?' he called. 'Adam Grant?' The people from Castle Dreich lay flat in the darkness, one of them directly under the window, as the policeman shone his torch into the bushes. But the light didn't land on anyone. It never occurred to the policeman that there were others more desperate to find Adam than he was.

Horrified, Mr Macleod sat on the bed where Adam had been. 'Why is this happening to me?'

'Don't worry, sir,' said the other policeman. 'We've dealt with difficult kids before.' Teenagers were an annoyance not really worth bothering with. 'They'll be back by morning.'

A sudden burst of music sang from Megan's pocket. Her phone was ringing. She showed Adam the name as she answered.

'Megan, it's Oliver. We're all really worried about you. Will you be coming back? Where are you?'

Megan thought fast. 'Oliver, I've found Adam,' she said. 'We're on the road back to the hostel.'

Adam gave Megan a thumbs-up and nodded.

'See you soon,' she said. The line went dead. 'Not likely,' she added.

Adam laughed wryly, surprised at how – in the midst of such chaos – he could still think of how much he liked looking at Megan's face.

Ahead, he could see a bungalow that was in darkness, the residents either out or asleep. They dashed across the road and into the back garden. Adam went over to a shed, regretting that his footprints left a pattern in the snow, but delighted when it was open. He beckoned Megan over and, perching between a mower and shelves of jam jars holding rusty nails, he leaned towards her. 'Here we are again, in a shed, in trouble.'

Megan explained her deduction, and Adam described how he had been chased, both interrupting the other to speculate why – 'why? why? why?' – all this could be happening.

Adam decided to call his parents on Megan's phone. His mother answered, but then the phone was taken by his father, who was not sympathetic. 'Adam, this is rather silly. We do understand that things have been difficult, but you need to come home now.'

'But, Dad,' Adam pleaded, 'something bad is happening. There were these people—'

'Listen,' Mr Grant said, slightly too loudly, making Adam wince – his father was rarely annoyed and that made it so much worse when it did happen. 'We're really worried. You haven't been yourself and you just need to get yourself back here as soon as possible.'

Adam closed his eyes. 'OK. OK. I promise.'

As soon as he ended the call, the phone rang again. *OLIVER* was the name that lit up the screen.

'Yes?' said Megan, suspicion creeping into her voice.

Oliver sounded different, agitated and hostile rather than his usual quiet self. 'Let's stop playing games. You're involved in something far, far bigger than you realize. We just want to look after Adam. We're the *last* people who want to hurt him, believe me.'

'We're going to the police.' Megan was matter-of-fact.

'They're not going to believe a word of it,' Oliver continued. 'And Adam can hardly stay under police guard forever? People will get hurt if you don't cooperate.'

Adam grabbed the phone and swore into it, telling Oliver where he could stick it. He pressed the End Call button aggressively. 'Sorry, Meg,' he said, 'but I think I made myself clear.'

Megan switched her phone off. It wasn't just to avoid calls – she also remembered hearing that it was possible to trace someone's location from their phone. And they had no idea how many people in the area were involved.

It was a bitterly cold night. The moon was waning, but the stars were clear and bright.

'We can't stay out here,' said Adam. 'We'll freeze.' He looked at the house, seeing its open curtains. 'I don't think anyone is in. Stay here, Meg, and keep watch.'

Adam went to the back of the bungalow and peered in. He could just about make out a tidy sitting room through one window and a double bed in another, neatly made. Then he went around to the front of the house. Listening carefully for any noise, he raced to the front door, drawn by a package poking out of the letter box; pushing open the flap, he saw a pile of other post.

'Meg, they're away. There's a heap of mail waiting,'

he said breathlessly on his return to the shed. 'Look, we're going to get inside and spend the night in there.'

'Break in?' said Megan doubtfully.

'Yes, break in. You know what Asa says: *Desperate times call for desperate measures.* Well, this is pretty bloody desperate. Worst case, we're arrested. I can live with that.'

Breaking in quietly was more difficult than Adam expected. Even without his injured shoulder, he probably couldn't force any of the windows, didn't dare smash them for fear of the noise, and the door was secure and double-glazed.

Megan was rustling around by some plants.

'Meg, can you help?' Adam whispered. 'If we can just get this plastic fixing to snap . . .'

Megan didn't answer.

'Meg? Meg! What are you doing?!' Adam asked, still at work on the fixing.

Something cold pressed against Adam's cheek, and he looked up to see Megan's grinning face. 'Spare key,' she said. 'It was worth looking. My grandparents put theirs under a plant pot. It was hidden behind that water butt.'

The key opened the door and they slipped past four bikes, one with stabilizers, and into the sitting room. Once the front curtains were drawn, Adam sat on the sofa, relieved to be in the relative warmth of the house.

Megan explored the kitchen, then joined him in the darkness. 'We're going to have to steal food, Adam,' she said.

Adam yawned. 'And nick their bikes probably. We'll have to put things right afterwards.' He pulled a cushion off the sofa and lay it on the floor. 'I don't think I'd be able to sleep in their beds.'

Megan also pulled down a cushion, and a blanket from the arm of the sofa.

Adam lay down against the sofa, with Megan in front of him, facing in the same direction. He put his left arm round her, flinching slightly at a twinge of pain, and she wriggled back slightly to be next to him, her hair resting against his face. He breathed out once, all of his fears disappearing, and fell asleep immediately.

Bolleskine did not sleep that night. His cars and people roamed every street in Aviemore, far more thorough than the police.

'We're going to watch all the roads, and the bus and railway station,' he said. 'Adam will not leave this town without us knowing.'

CHAPTER 19

'HELP'
(MONDAY 15TH DECEMBER 2014)

On their way to continue the hunt for Adam, several Toyota Land Cruisers with winter tyres rumbled out of the garage at Castle Dreich.

Abbie, standing with a small group at the bottom of the main steps, wanted to catch her father's eye as he drove past, but he was looking ahead, serious and resolute, and didn't even glance her way. Bolleskine's eyes met Abbie's and didn't waver.

'Once the boy is here, then we will be ready,' someone said.

Abbie listened carefully. If ever there was a chance to escape, it was now.

After six weeks at Castle Dreich, Abbie was used to the distinction between the Inner Guard and the Pillars. The Pillars were cooks, administrators and those responsible for recruiting new members. The Inner Guard, which now included her father, consisted of those closest to Bolleskine. There used to be a third group, the Inclined, but this group had withered to nothing: new members were not being

133

recruited now, and those already in the castle were getting more serious.

Abbie was guided into the castle by a wiry woman in her fifties, one of the Inner Guard. Abbie decided to take a chance, to risk saying something that assumed more knowledge than she really had. 'Will the boy they're getting be put with the others?' she asked.

'Adam is exceptional. He will be given exceptional treatment.' The woman had a mouth that looked as if it was trying to smile but the rest of her face wouldn't allow it. 'He will lead us. Adam is the hundredth and final traveller.'

'I know that. I *have* been listening.' But there were things Abbie didn't know. 'How do we travel?'

The woman spoke earnestly. 'We will be guided across time and space.'

Abbie looked away from the castle into the night. It was miles to the road, and then ten or twenty more miles to the nearest village. 'Will there be some sort of *spaceship*?'

She was full of simple trust: 'We will be taken.'

This was going round in circles. 'By what method of transport?' *By what vehicle, you idiot? HOW?*

'That is not for me to say or you to know. But our spirits will be taken.'

Spirits? 'What about our bodies?'

The woman squinted slightly, trying not to say too much. 'They will be left here.' And after a pause, to make it clear she really hadn't given anything away, she added, 'Of course.'

The words tumbled from Abbie: 'You mean we're all going to commit suicide?'

The woman slapped Abbie hard once, then, as Abbie recovered and stood upright again, another slap, even harder. Her eyes were dark and livid. 'We will be liberated and free from this world,' she said. 'We will live on. Those who are left will see this world as it truly is.'

Abbie had felt depressed and worried; now shock, panic and terror rose above the pain in her cheek.

She had to escape.

It took five of them to hold Abbie down. She spat and swore even after each limb had been restrained and her head was gripped tight between someone's knees.

'Open your mouth!' It was the same woman. 'Open your mouth!'

Abbie saw a hand coming towards her, with the yellow crumbly drug that smelt like pepper, pinched between fingers protected by a plastic glove. She pushed her lips tight together. But her nose was held, and her lips were being forced open, and she was being punched in the stomach, and . . .

She couldn't resist any longer. The crumbs went into her mouth.

Delivery by water, even in tiny doses, generated suspicious fear and vague, confused imaginings. When injected, the effect was immediate: hallucinations. As gas, it took effect gradually. Taken as a solid, the outcome was different again: there was a delay, then sudden and terrible visions – so real that they could be touched.

More than a teaspoon, taken in any form, resulted in death. Abbie swallowed about half that amount, far more than she ever had before.

A huge spider came to her, brushed its hairy leg across her face and forced her to stand up. Abbie's body was rigid with horror and disgust.

Abbie realized that the drug did not confuse. It seemed completely normal that a spider was wrapping its front legs around her shoulders and forcing her to help in the kitchen.

It whispered in her ear.

Tick, tick.

Tick, tick.

The real world was still normal, unaffected: spices on

a shelf, cinnamon, black pepper, and other flavourings. On one hob a pot of pasta simmered gently. Hundreds of peeled potatoes sat in enormous metal saucepans. And a spider rested its abdomen against her back.

'These are for the cavern.' Pasta was being spooned into plastic containers. 'Abbie, put them on a tray.'

Abbie was tense, trying not to press against the spider. She knew it wasn't there – *it isn't there – it isn't there – it isn't there – it isn't there – it isn't there* – yet it was.

Maybe it was there.

No – it isn't, she thought.

Yes, I am, its fangs clicked.

Hallucination!

'Abbie, put these on a tray!' The voice was louder.

The kitchen was a flurry of activity as Abbie brought over the tray. She placed the containers on them one by one. The notepad in front of her said that there should be twelve.

She had an idea. No one was looking at her except the spider, which shrieked and shot out silk, wrapping it around Abbie's face; it dug its fangs into her neck.

It didn't stop her.

In the caverns below, a boy poked at his pasta. He was called Max, and had been selected as a scientist to be taken on the cult's journey. *I must keep my strength up*, he thought.

After a couple of mouthfuls he realized that something else was in the container. At first he thought it was a piece of plastic, but turning his pasta over with his fork, he plucked out a tiny piece of pencil – and there was a small piece of paper as well.

Who are you? I want to help.

Max held the paper to his chest, then slid it in his pocket. As he had many times since his arrival, he wept. He looked up at the ceiling, glancing at the cameras, wondering what the consequences of discovery would be.

The spider was smaller and less tactile when the trays returned.

'Abbie, sort this out, please. Throw away the leftovers, wash the containers,' said the woman.

'Of course.' Abbie meant it to sound helpful, but it still came out like a teenager's grudging acceptance of work.

The last container was nearly full. She dribbled the contents into the bin slowly.

Then she saw the slip of paper. She touched it. It was real – not a hallucination. Max had only risked four letters.

HELP

CHAPTER 20

LEAVING AVIEMORE
(TUESDAY 16TH DECEMBER 2014)

Adam lay awake, enjoying having his arm around Megan. He seemed not to have moved at all in the night.

Megan had been awake for longer and noticed that Adam's breath on her ear had changed in rhythm. 'Are you awake?' she asked.

Blurred reality suddenly clicked into focus for Adam. 'We need to go.' But he tightened his hold on Megan slightly. 'I have a plan, and it starts with borrowing as much breakfast as we can.'

Aviemore is a busy place after snowfall in the holiday season, so the people from Castle Dreich had no problem blending in. Abbie's father, Mark, stamped his feet on the ground as he stood with another man outside the railway station, glancing at each person that passed, scrutinizing the face of anyone in black ski jacket and salopettes. Adam had not gone by. Mark sent a text to the men at the bus station and received one back seconds later: *Nothing here either.*

A heavy lorry threw up slush on to a Land Cruiser parked in a lay-by on the A9 Edinburgh road. More men sat watching the A9 going in the other direction, north, next to a sign marked *Inverness*.

Bolleskine circled the town of Aviemore – a wolf trying to smell out his prey. 'If he leaves, he will head south: the lure of home. The *supposed* safety of Edinburgh.'

Adam was pointing at a road atlas that they had found in the kitchen. 'Edinburgh's the capital. There'll be police there who know about this sort of thing, who might even know who *we* are. Or we can get the train home –' Adam's finger ran down the map of Britain that was on the inside cover – 'to London.'

'We need to get the local police involved,' said Megan. 'They can trace Oliver – and then track down the cars.'

'Yes, but there's no way I'm going to hand myself to the local guys, who'll just force me to go back to Mr Macleod. And there are several of those Toyota Land Cruisers.' Adam glanced at a picture on the mantelpiece in the sitting room and pointed. 'He's about my age, isn't he? No wonder that mountain bike's my size. Maybe you can use one of the adult ones?'

They spent about ten minutes discussing their options.

Adam was animated, and Megan added her own ideas, dangerous though Adam thought they were.

He was adjusting the seat on one of the bikes, his mouth full of dry cornflakes, when there was a rattle at the front door and the bell rang. They crouched down close to the floor and froze. The bell rang again and there was another short burst of knocking. In the silence that followed, they could hear an engine outside. Adam saw the kitchen knives nearby, but shoved the thought from his mind.

Then came the higher-pitched sound of a car pulling away, and Adam ran and put his eye to a small opening between the curtains. A red Royal Mail van was driving off.

'Let's get a move on,' said Adam. 'I'm terrified the people who live here are going to return. Are you with me?'

Megan kissed him. Her answer was clear.

Abbie's father called Bolleskine the moment he saw the black salopettes and ski jacket cycling towards the station. 'He's about 400 yards away, just getting off a bike, using a mobile.'

HELP, came in the message to the police telephone operator, *I'm a child in danger at Aviemore station. There's a man after me. He wants to hurt me.*

Child, man, hurt: the key words triggered an immediate response. Two police cars closed in – as did the Toyota Land Cruisers.

The train was due to leave Aviemore for Edinburgh at 13:31. It was 1.25 p.m., just before it pulled into the station.

1.26 P.M.

Sirens could be heard swirling in the distance as the police fought to get to the station in time. Toyota Land Cruisers drew up and parked outside the station.

Megan repeated her message: *Please help. I'm going to be attacked.*

1.27 P.M.

Less than 250 yards from the train door. The bike, wheeled along, cut through black slush at the side of the road. Nervous short breaths panted through a scarf.

1.28 P.M.

Abbie's father touched the syringe in his pocket. It contained the same drug that had been forced into Abbie. 'Let us make it so,' said Bolleskine into his telephone.

'Wait until he's level with you and then strike – we'll steer him down a side street and get him into a car.'

1.29 P.M.

Just 125 yards from the train; one minute's walk, and then Abbie's father could administer the drug.

1.30 P.M.

Police cars came to a halt and officers stepped out.

Three paces ahead of Abbie's father.

'Help me!' shouted Megan, appealing to a policewoman. She ripped off her scarf and tore down the hood of Adam's jacket. 'I'm the girl who's been calling.' She grabbed the arm of the officer. 'And take down that number plate.' Pulling away into the distance was the same Land Cruiser that Megan had been crouching behind the night before.

1.31 P.M.

The train doors closed.

EARLIER THAT DAY

'Right. Let's get our kit off!'

'Adam!'

'Here,' Adam continued, 'I'll put these on.' He held up

jeans and a rather sickly-looking green coat that belonged to the boy who lived in the house.

Megan put on Adam's black ski jacket and salopettes; Adam discovered that the boy was a bit taller than he was, but probably about the same around the waist. The green coat had a cinema ticket in the pocket, and the presence of a personal item made the borrowing feel like *stealing*.

'You'll need to make sure they can't see your face,' Adam said.

Megan wrote a note for the people who lived in the house:

> *Dear family,*
> *You have helped us without knowing it. We didn't*
> *have a choice.*
> > *Many thanks – we'll repay you when we can.*
> > *From two grateful kids*
> *PS We have borrowed all £35 from the kitchen jar,*
> *some clothes, a little food and two bikes.*

Adam was right about one thing. The roads were being watched.

It was seven miles from Aviemore to Carrbridge, the next railway station north. 'One of Europe's great wildernesses,'

Mr Macleod had said, and Adam appreciated that rugged isolation as he bumped and slid along the slushy road.

The plan was for him to go north, further away from Edinburgh, get on a train at Carrbridge railway station, and then come back south. The railway line went back through Aviemore, but by then he would be on the train, keeping his head down, while Megan distracted everyone.

The problem wasn't simply that the road was icy, it was that the snow was so unpredictable. Adam could see why his dad said Eskimos have over fifty words for it – some snow helped traction, some was wet and heavy, and some crisp and covered in ice. A string of swear words spilt from Adam as he slipped and slithered, fighting to keep the bike upright.

He had expected the whole journey to take him little over an hour, but progress was much slower, so he was beginning to get worried about the time – and then he saw a Toyota Land Cruiser in the distance. It was parked by the side of the road on a snow-covered verge.

Adam lay the bike flat and ducked down, thumping the snowy tarmac in frustration. He looked at the forest that was thick on either side of the road. Safer, but much slower – and he had to get the right train, otherwise the plan wouldn't work.

It would be hopeless to try to race past: even at little more than jogging pace the bike was nearly impossible to control. They would easily catch him.

During this indecision, Adam heard an engine approaching, about to emerge over the brow of a hill about 150 yards behind him. He would have to take his chance in the forest after all.

But as he reached the trees he realized that what was coming up the road was much larger than a 4x4. A yellow metal neck came first, followed by the body of a JCB, a snowplough on the front scraping as it went.

Adam acted before his plan properly made sense. He dashed out as the JCB trundled past, leaped on the bike, grabbed the shovel at the back of the truck with his left hand, and hid behind the yellow arm as best he could, fighting with all his strength to keep the front wheel of the bike straight, his legs locked into the frame.

And he was pulled along. Now there was no swearing: Adam gritted his teeth as his body screamed in protest.

Hidden from view on the far side of the JCB, he passed the Toyota Land Cruiser.

He managed to keep hold for over half a mile, a feat achieved more through persistence than judgement, until the front wheel turned to the right on a patch of ice, the bike twisted under him and he fell to the ground, again on to his left side. Pain's jagged bolts punched through him.

He was now much closer to Carrbridge, and the road was easier and clearer now that the snowplough had passed ahead of him. Having the bike was vital, and, sweating and exhausted, his left side dull with pain, he pedalled hard up the hill to get to the station on time.

He hid the bike in some bushes behind the station, boarded the train and eight minutes later was back in Aviemore. He looked out from his seat, unable to resist a glance, and was just about able to see Megan talking to a policewoman. He saw three or four people wander nonchalantly away. The doors locked, and the train started to accelerate, the guard announcing that its final destination would be Edinburgh Waverley Station.

'As if by magic,' Adam muttered. 'Well done, Meg.'

It was another two hours and forty-five minutes to Edinburgh.

CHAPTER 21

NO ESCAPE
(TUESDAY 16TH DECEMBER 2014)

It was late in the evening when they came to get Abbie. She was craning her head out of the window, thinking about the layout of the castle, when the door opened without warning and two people entered.

One was the woman who seemed to have been entrusted with Abbie's 'welfare'. Abbie had heard her being called Vee, but she didn't know what that was short for, nor what her surname was. Surnames were rarely used in Castle Dreich – the idea was that everyone was now one family. Vee's fanaticism worried Abbie; her belief seemed absolute.

The man with her was Alistair – Abbie loathed his pinched, pale face more than ever. Whereas Abbie could imagine that Vee was a reasonable, if peculiar, person in the outside world, Alistair was a wasp of a man. He was often with Bolleskine, snivelling and whispering, spinning his nastiness. Abbie felt as if she was allergic to him.

'Abbie, come with us,' snarled Alistair. 'We have something to show you.'

'I'd rather stay here, if you don't mind,' said Abbie in a low tone. She still saw hints of spiders in the corners of the room and was sure there was one in the corridor outside. Knowing that they were hallucinations didn't help. The drug was too powerful.

'No,' he barked, 'it's not an invitation; it's an instruction.'

Abbie wondered what Alistair had been before he came to Castle Dreich. Probably a teacher who enjoyed making kids cry, or an inflexible traffic warden sticking tickets on disabled people's cars, a small man desperate for power and the opportunity to be disgusting.

'OK,' said Abbie. 'I'm cooperating now.' She stood up to show her willingness.

'We wouldn't want to punish you,' leered Alistair.

I bet you would, thought Abbie.

'Come along . . . or we'll have to teach you a lesson,' he whispered, staring, eyes like marbles behind thick glasses.

Abbie was led down through the building, emerging on to the central staircase, off which there were rooms big enough to host many people, as well as one that was a large sitting room.

At the bottom of the stairs was the front door.

'Look,' said Vee. She pulled back a bolt and clicked up an old-fashioned latch. Wind blew the door open an inch. 'No lock to stop you getting out.'

Abbie's mind began to whirl. She had assumed that there would be extensive security.

'Of course,' said Alistair, his reedy voice sarcastic and dismissive, regardless of the words, 'we know when the door is opened, and there's other security in the valley, but everything is designed to keep people *out*.'

Vee locked and unlocked the door again to show that it wasn't a trick. 'Always the same.'

Abbie stretched out her hand and pulled open the large wooden door. It was heavy and solid, but well-oiled and opened easily. Light from the castle shone about twenty yards across the track that swept past the front door and alongside the loch. At its end, Abbie knew, was the main road.

'Let's go out into the darkness.' Alistair gestured towards the open door.

'I'm not going out there with you,' said Abbie, ready to fight, considering a dash for freedom. 'No way.' They would have to pin her down again and force far more of the drug into her before she went anywhere with him.

Vee stepped out and wandered to the edge of the gloom. 'Come with *me* then,' she suggested, holding out her hand. It was the hand that had slapped Abbie yesterday.

Abbie forced herself on, step by step, both terrified and intrigued, hoping to learn as much as she could. She could hear Alistair's sniffing behind her; perhaps an occasional chuckle.

At the edge of the darkness, Vee grabbed Abbie's arm and Alistair pushed himself next to her, pinning her tight. 'You slimy bastard,' Abbie said instinctively.

He ignored her. 'Now,' he said, 'stretch out your hand into the darkness.'

Abbie pushed her hand forward, the only sound her slow deep breaths. At first, there was nothing, then, a little further on, she felt . . . She wasn't sure. *A branch. Maybe a tree?*

'Go on,' Alistair said in her ear. 'See what it is.'

What? Abbie thought. *It's got thorns. A bush?*

But there were no trees near the castle.

Then something soft. Hair. A tooth.

No – fangs.

'I know what it is,' said Abbie, 'and I don't want to stay here any more.'

'Say the word,' taunted Alistair.

'S-spi-spider.' *I must be as hard as nails*, thought Abbie.

'You see what a horrible world we live in,' said Vee.

151

'We must escape these demons and go to the promised place.'

'And you're wrong,' said Alistair. 'Not *a* spider.' His face was turned towards Abbie, spittle glistening on his lips. 'Spiders.'

He pushed Abbie forward into spiders that swarmed around her: small spiders ticked across her skin and were caught in her hair, larger spiders clung to her legs and arms, and the largest of all were like thick bushes and curtains, hemming her in, nudging her from side to side.

'None of this is happening,' shouted Abbie as she tore and spun around in the darkness. 'It's not real!' But the drug coursed through the blood vessels in her brain, tiny pellets of poison, turning the darkness into her greatest fear.

Smothered in spiders, she could see a dull light and lunged awkwardly towards it, falling into Alistair's waiting arms. 'Get off me,' she screamed, pushing him away and stumbling back towards the castle door, then running inside.

'You see why we don't lock the door,' Alistair laughed after her. 'Sleep well!'

Vee turned to Alistair. 'Don't be too hard on her,

Alistair. She doesn't realize what an evil place this world is and how desperately we need to escape it.'

'I think she does,' said Alistair, smiling as Abbie ran up the stairs. 'But give her more of our medicine. Let her see things *very* clearly.'

CHAPTER 22

OLIVER VS ADAM
(TUESDAY 16TH DECEMBER 2014)

The police could tell immediately that Megan was not like the troublesome teenagers they usually dealt with.

'Look,' she said, 'this is a major incident.' Even the words *major incident* sounded peculiar from a fifteen-year-old. 'Please just stop that man over there, the one walking towards the Land Cruiser.' Megan was careful not to overstate her case. 'Just talk to him, don't arrest him. He's the man who was after me.' She pointed, desperate.

Abbie's father was opening the passenger door when the police called to him to stop.

'Thank you,' said Megan, seeing light at the end of the tunnel. 'Don't forget that number plate, and make sure you get that one as well.' She pointed firmly at the 4x4 just ahead of them.

'Thank you, *madam*,' said a policeman, who then jogged towards the Land Cruiser, calling for it to stop.

Abbie's father was just about to get in. 'Is there anything I can do for you, officer?'

'We've received a report that you've been acting

suspiciously.' The officer, peering in the car, saw two other men, one of them Bolleskine. 'Can you tell us what you're doing here, sir?'

Bolleskine raised his eyebrows in surprise at the question.

Abbie's father also looked innocent. 'A bit of skiing, we hope, if the snow stays.'

'And why were you out of the car?'

He pulled energy drinks out of his pocket and chuckled. 'We're not as young as we used to be!'

'Can I see some ID, sir?'

Mark Hopkins had been waiting for this. 'Yes, I think so.' He pulled a wallet out of his jacket and removed a card rather like a driving licence.

At the top left, the ID card had a golden sea lion surrounded by roses and portcullises, with the words *Regnum Defende* underneath, then *MI5 The Security Service*. 'I've been in the service for over twenty years,' he said, half apologetically. He looked carefully at the police officer, who had been joined by a colleague. 'If there's any trouble, I'll be sure to let you know. Please do take down my service number –' he pointed at a long series of numbers and letters at the top right – 'and the number plate of this car.'

The policeman looked back at Megan and then at Commander Mark Hopkins, MI5 Intelligence Officer Grade 10.

Megan could see that there was a complication.

'Perhaps calling a number will clear things up?' suggested Commander Hopkins casually. 'Do you have a pen?' It was a London number, someone in Thames House who would vouch for him.

Megan turned to the policewoman by her side. 'What can be taking so long?' she said in a high-pitched, slightly frantic voice. 'The others are getting away.' She could see the policeman using his mobile phone. Megan moved a little closer to the policewoman. 'There's a boy involved in this as well – he's called Oliver Arkwright.'

To Megan's horror, the policeman started smiling at the people in the car. 'What?' she said. 'Why is he just letting them go?'

She realized that if they had been let go, Adam was again in danger. She turned to the policewoman. 'Adam Grant, the missing boy, is on the train that has just left. You need to get police officers to him as soon as possible.'

Adam was relieved when the train pulled away from Aviemore with no one who looked dangerous having

156

boarded. Before long he would be in Edinburgh, could walk into a major police station and maybe mention some of the senior police officers he had dealt with in the aftermath of the previous Christmas.

The Scottish countryside slid past as the train headed to the next station, Kingussie. The track was hemmed in by frosty mountains on both sides. Adam saw a couple of lochs and the blue thread of the River Spey on his left, but his thoughts were back in Aviemore, outside the railway station with Megan. He pictured the handcuffing of snarling criminals, with Megan directing proceedings, and he smiled.

A Scottish announcer interrupted his imaginings. 'The next station is Kingussie.' Adam saw that it was a very small town, with about ten people dotted along the platform. He sank deep into his seat.

At the far end, where Adam couldn't quite see, was Oliver. With him was a tall, slim man with a large birthmark on his left cheek and glasses balanced on his thin nose. He had been pacing up and down the platform, looking carefully at the waiting passengers; he now kept a close eye on the entrance. When the train arrived, Oliver's job was to quickly search the carriages, starting at the front of the train.

Oliver saw no one in the first carriage even vaguely like Adam: families sat restlessly while other travellers concentrated on books or gazed out the window.

Then Oliver checked the second carriage, looking carefully at everyone.

Another boy stared back, confusion and annoyance immediately combining and multiplying. 'What you looking at?' he said to Oliver in a no-nonsense Glaswegian accent as he yanked headphones from his ears. 'Have you got a problem?'

Oliver looked carefully at him for two or three seconds, then lost interest and went to the third and final carriage. About half the places were occupied – but it was easy to spot Adam low in his seat, looking out of the window. Oliver ducked back and beckoned to Alistair to join him, but at that moment the doors bleeped and closed, leaving Alistair slapping his hand against the window as the train pulled away.

Adam looked up towards the noise of the man trying to get on and spotted an innocent-looking pale-faced boy with blond hair: Oliver.

The train was gathering speed.

Adam glanced at the door between the carriages, then looked back at Oliver and cagily said, 'Hi.' He reckoned that Oliver wouldn't start a fight on a train.

The train was rattling along past snow-covered fields as Oliver came towards Adam, muttering into his mobile phone with one hand and reaching in his pocket with the other. 'We don't want to hurt you,' he said as he put the phone away, 'we want to *help* you.'

There were some wary looks from other passengers, but they were not about to get involved in an altercation between two teenagers.

'I thought you were my friend,' said Adam. 'I trusted you.'

'You are a very important person,' Oliver replied. 'You just don't see it. Yet.'

As Oliver reached for the syringe, Adam stood up, pushing Oliver's arm away and shoulder-barging him towards the seats opposite, where he fell on to a man reading a newspaper.

Most passengers now made sure that they were busily occupied, but one elderly lady shouted, 'You boys should behave yourselves!'

Adam pressed the button to open the doors between the carriages, swaying slightly with the movement of the train, as Oliver disentangled himself from the man and ignored his complaints.

Moving forward into the middle carriage of the train, Adam realized that he would soon run out of places to go. Perhaps he could lock himself in the toilet. But as Adam approached, he saw a red engaged sign.

Oliver was now in the same carriage.

'Just leave me alone!' said Adam.

Oliver came closer, halfway through the carriage, as Adam retreated again. 'I'm doing the right thing for *you*,' said Oliver, ignoring the people around them, not noticing that he nudged the Scottish boy as the train wobbled. The needle was now visible in his hand.

The Glaswegian took his headphones off again and bristled aggressively. 'Hey, you.'

Oliver didn't seem to hear.

The train was at its full speed as Adam went through into the front carriage, nearest the driver. At the next station he could leap out and get help. He urged the train on.

Oliver followed Adam, reaching the interconnecting doors just as they closed. He pressed impatiently. But as he entered and looked immediately to the far end, Adam was nowhere to be seen.

THUMP.

Adam's fist made solid contact with Oliver's cheek.

Leaping off the seat immediately to the left of the door, Adam made a grab for the needle with his left hand and thumped wildly with his right.

Oliver was far more muscular than Adam had thought; he was wriggling furiously and Adam realized that he was not going to be able to hold him. So he put everything he had into one shove, leaving him between the seats, and then retreated back into the middle carriage.

Three or four people stood up to intervene, and one of them called after Adam, yelling at him to stop as he raced down the aisle.

Adam felt the train begin to slow. It was only five minutes between Kingussie and Newtonmore stations, and there was a slight squeak of brakes as Oliver entered the middle carriage.

'Just stay away from me,' Adam shouted. He saw houses outside now – the station must be near.

The Glaswegian stood up as Adam passed him, and faced Oliver, who was following. 'I've told you more than once.'

Adam now saw what Oliver could do in a straight scrap. As other passengers looked on, stunned, Oliver held himself slightly off the floor between the seats and jabbed his foot into the taller boy's stomach, shunting him backwards. But the Scottish boy had been in fights before; the livid fog of anger enveloped him and he was determined to do some damage to Oliver.

The train was slowing down.

'Hey, stop it!' said another passenger, and two stocky men in their early twenties entered from the front carriage, cornering Oliver.

For a few moments it was as if the scene was freeze-framed. Oliver weighed up the odds, glancing at those around him; Adam urged the seconds on, looking between Oliver and the train doors.

The doors opened. Adam shoved past a family waiting to get on and glanced back briefly: there was a scuffle on board. A few seconds later, briefly pausing at the end of the platform, he could see Oliver halfway off the train, the Scottish boy holding on to him. Adam frantically looked around for a place to hide.

Should he try the car park? Or would his pursuers be arriving? Maybe the fields on the far side of the train?

A variety of shouts came from the carriage, some of them aimed at Adam. The family who had been about to get on cowered, their young son clinging to his mother's side.

Through the chaos, for an instant, Oliver's eyes met Adam's. Then Adam was gone.

Oliver shoved back his head, thrust down his foot into the Scottish boy's knee, and lashed out with his elbow. His opponent slumped to the floor.

Adam ran across the tracks behind the train and vaulted the fence on the far side, landing in a drift of damp snow. He started to run at an angle across the fields, towards a line of trees.

Oliver jabbed his needle towards those nearest to him and shouted, 'Get away from me!'

The police, already alerted by Megan, were given greater urgency to reach the scene by a flurry of 999 calls.

But Bolleskine was already on his way.

CHAPTER 23

HIDE AND SEEK
(TUESDAY 16TH DECEMBER 2014)

Lifting his feet high, arms outstretched for balance, Adam ran through the field. The snow wasn't deep, perhaps only two or three inches, but it made every stride unpredictable and treacherous. The train, which had been held in the station, fell into the distance, and Adam was slightly over halfway towards the trees when he saw a figure pursuing him. He could just about see that it was Oliver, hand pressed to ear, probably using a mobile phone.

Although he was out of breath and slightly dizzy when he reached the trees, his legs were still fresh. Oliver could follow his footprints across open ground, but he couldn't do that under a canopy of trees.

To his dismay, the wood was less extensive than he had thought, just one or two trees wide, but he followed them rather than running straight out.

Oliver paused as he entered the trees. Adam had anticipated Oliver's dilemma: Adam could be hiding – or could be about to double back – or could have run off at any angle – or maybe he had run straight out the other side.

'Adam?' Oliver shouted. 'Adam? *Please!* We want to help you!'

Adam heard the shouting in the distance as he emerged on to a fairly wide and very long field. For an instant he couldn't work it out: then the indentations and dotted flags made sense: it was a snow-covered golf course.

'Adam?' Oliver shouted again.

The sound of his name spurred Adam on. He headed up and across the fairway towards a longer and more dense-looking wood.

Then far away in front of him, he saw two figures. Frustrated golfers? Police? Friends of Oliver? Adam halted. Looking over his shoulder he could again see Oliver, maybe three hundred yards distant.

Faintly on the breeze, he heard his name once more.

Soon he was in woodland again, twisting and leaping, running wildly and less successfully, panic urging him on. For a time he wasn't sure which direction he was going, but at least there was no way anyone could have followed such an erratic path.

Ahead was the sound of gushing water.

'Adam?' It was Oliver, closer than he thought.

'Adam?' An adult's voice, somewhere behind him.

Both voices came again, closer still.

Adam darted forward towards the water – as three people closed in through the wood.

Adam came to a halt. The River Spey, wide and freezing-cold, was dancing over rocks in front of him. It looked too broad to cross easily. But he could now see Oliver and two other men, spread out, cutting off any escape back through the wood.

'ADAM! We don't want to hurt you – as you will see . . .' said Oliver.

Adam looked at the river. He had no idea how cold it was, and knew little about hypothermia beyond the name, but he could see the tops of lorries passing on the far side. If he could just get to that road, someone would rescue him.

The three were now no more than a few paces away. They all had needles. If it had only been Oliver, Adam would have thumped him and risked an injection, but three of them, and two of them adults . . . So, as Oliver started to say something, Adam turned and ran into the water, then dived forward, narrowly missing scraping his face along the bottom.

He had never experienced such a sudden rush of cold before. It immediately wrapped itself around him, stinging him, smothering him, drawing out his breath and replacing it with ice. He felt desperately thin – that his insides were shrinking away to nothing. He managed about six strokes of front crawl, sometimes also able to push off against the bottom, before he began to shiver. He also realized that he was being dragged downriver by the current, a force that was far stronger than his weakening efforts.

Adam was too cold to think properly, but deep inside himself he knew that he had made the wrong decision. A rush of panic – the fear that he was going to die – joined the intense cold.

Burning within him, fighting back, was the fierce desire to survive.

Just at that point, Adam felt something stony knock against his knee, and he put his hand into mud on the far side of the river.

It took all his strength for him to stand – his clothes were dripping wet, sticking to him like an iron wrap. He shivered vigorously as he fought to take his top off. *Get the cold clothes off*, he thought, *otherwise you'll die.*

The three had followed him downstream back on the far bank. They were talking to one another and looking across at Adam.

'Y-you w-w-won't catch me, b-b-bastards,' shouted Adam as best he could. 'Ha!'

His T-shirt wouldn't quite go over his head, but then it was free. He tried to wipe the water off his chest, doubled over with shivering, his face contorted as he fought against the cold spears that twisted inside him. Now he had to get to the road.

On the other side, one of the men looked up. Adam followed his line of sight. He had seen something in the air. Adam picked out the same object: a helicopter.

Adam waved his hands feebly. 'Help! Help!' He stood as much like a star as he could, trying to force his legs and arms wide. 'I'm here!' he croaked.

The helicopter had seen him and was moving at speed. *Stay where you are*, Adam thought, trying to focus on the other three while his head jogged up and down with cold.

Then Adam used his damp feet to try to spell out *HELP* in the snow, but he had only managed part of the *H* when he realized no more letters were needed: the helicopter was coming lower, making a direct line for him.

Oliver and the other two stood their ground.

Suddenly Adam's hope dulled. Why were the others not running away? Adam was unable to see any markings on the helicopter apart from the registration number – nothing saying *Police*.

Flecks of snow were thrown in the air as it circled and

then began to descend behind Adam. He was forced to the ground by the terrible gale thrown out from the rotors, hugging himself in an attempt to keep warm. Then, through slits of eyes, he saw that the men inside didn't have uniforms, and that the helicopter looked old.

He tried to stumble away, and lashed out as someone came towards him. Then there was another: one man on each arm. Something warm was being put over him.

'You bastards,' he muttered as he passed out.

CHAPTER 24

PRISON
(TUESDAY 16TH DECEMBER 2014)

Adam looked around at his prison. It was like being trapped inside a huge jam jar. Adam thought of ships in bottles, but this was squarer, like an old-fashioned telephone box but bigger, made completely of thick panes of glass fastened together by strong metal strips. There were metal fixings that screwed the whole container tightly to the floor – presumably it had been lowered over him and then attached. He looked up through the transparent top. The cavern ceiling, high above, was jagged and looked a bit damp. But he wasn't cold – the containers were warmed by a slight breeze through a grate, a bit like a drain, beneath his feet.

Adam found he had been dressed in green and purple robes with plain shorts and a grey T-shirt underneath. On the robe by his heart there was a yellow circular badge with jagged lines coming out of it, but no belt, no buttons, nothing he could use to help him escape.

Adam was too stunned even to despair. *What is this place? Why am I here?* He held his hands against his head in frustration.

The cave was big and he could see he wasn't alone. There were twelve other containers, arranged in an X, each about five yards apart, with him as the centre point. Each container had someone inside. Two boys and two girls looked at him from the four closest boxes. They were all about his age.

'I'm Adam!' he shouted. 'Why are we here?' And again: 'Why are we here?' But the sound was trapped by the glass and sounded hollow.

They stared at him, giving no hint of communication. They looked scared.

Stay calm, he thought. *Use your brain.*

He tapped on the glass but knew that the others couldn't hear him. 'Hello?' His voice echoed dully. One boy gave a flicker of acknowledgement, so Adam tried again, forming his greeting carefully, making lip-reading easy. 'Hello?'

The boy looked down.

Adam thought about his prison again. Maybe they were in an old mine – they sometimes had huge chambers like this one – though it could be natural. Again he slapped his hands against the inside of the container.

The only noise came up through the grate, about eighteen inches square, beneath his feet. He could hear a trickle of water and, perhaps, the faintest of shouts from one of the other prisoners. The noise must be travelling through underground pipes. After shouting for help but getting no reply, he tried repeatedly and desperately to pull the grate up, but the fixings were too deep and too strong. It probably served one important purpose – the removal of human waste. But there was no privacy.

Adam examined the metal hatch, the only part of his prison that was not glass. On the outside there was a metal tray that could be slid in. Adam had seen something similar in a petrol station late at night: money was put in and then pushed through to the cashier. But this opening was no bigger than his hand, so even if Adam could force it open, he wouldn't be able to squeeze through.

He was thumping at it with the side of his fist in frustration when he saw two people approaching. One was a blonde good-looking girl, probably about sixteen; the other a woman in her fifties, thin, but muscular in a way that was unusual. The girl was obediently walking behind the woman, holding a tray with thirteen cartons of food, thirteen plastic bottles of water and thirteen plastic spoons.

'Hello, Adam,' the older woman said as she put one of the cartons on to the tray that was outside the hatch. Then she moved a switch and slid the tray into Adam's capsule. The meal looked a bit like airline food: meat in gravy, vegetables and potatoes.

'What's going on?' Adam shouted angrily through the hatch. 'You can't keep me here like this.' He swore.

'Everything will become clear,' said the woman.

Snorting with frustration, Adam took the food. Immediately the hatch slammed shut.

Adam looked at the girl carrying the tray. She was impassive, concentrating on the woman. Then, for an instant, she looked at Adam – and he saw her right eyelid close. Adam looked back to his food. But he had seen it. I *have* seen it, he convinced himself as he watched the girl walk away, up a handful of steps and through a door. The girl had winked. And there was something in the very slight flicker of her eyebrows that suggested to Adam they were on the same side.

Adam pressed his hand and face to the edge of his container and caught the attention of the girl in the next one. He waved slowly and expansively: 'Hello,' he mouthed.

The girl stared back, unmoving. He could see her mouth twitch a little. Perhaps that was a 'Hello'.

Adam pointed at his wrist, where his watch used to be.

'How long?' Then pointed to the floor. 'Here.'

The girl subtly pointed up and across, looking worried. Adam followed the direction of her finger and saw a CCTV camera fixed high on the cavern wall. He squinted into the gloom and could make out others.

No one here looked as if they had been beaten up, though they were obviously scared. In fact, since he had eaten, Adam had begun to feel the same sense of doom and hopelessness he had experienced on the way up to Scotland.

He peered at the camera. 'You can stick this up your arse,' he screamed, showing his middle finger, cheering himself slightly.

The other prisoners stared at Adam but they looked away whenever he caught their eyes.

Adam turned back to the girl, patiently waiting until she would look at him. 'How long have you been here?' he mouthed. Then more simply: 'How – long – here?'

The girl shrugged. She timidly held up both hands, fingers splayed. Then did the same again. And again. Then her hands covered her face as it crumpled.

Days or weeks? Adam didn't know. And it must be hard to keep track of time in the artificial light. He wondered how long he had been unconscious.

The girl in the container sat down and slumped against the glass, head lolling.

When she looked up again, Adam urged her to respond. He pushed his hands together: *please*. He pointed to his mouth: *talk*. He pointed to his chest: *to me*.

She shook her head a little.

Adam stepped back into the middle of his container and frowned. He put his hands out in front of him, miming being trapped inside a box. He frowned very obviously, then made great play of exploring the limits of the invisible barriers. Then the wide smile of understanding – an answer! He pretended to find an invisible handle and open an invisible door. Adam took one step forward and walked into the real barrier. It was as if he was trying to entertain a very small kid.

The girl smiled a little. Then she looked sad again.

Adam pointed to himself and mouthed: 'Ad'; then again: 'Am.'

Once more: 'Adam.'

She responded. 'Ell – En.' Then she stood up: 'Ell – En.'

Adam repeated it: 'Ellen?'

She shook her head and made exaggerated breaths, as if she was pretending to be a dragon breathing fire.

Ah. He understood. '*H*elen.'

She smiled and mouthed very deliberately: 'Hi, Adam.'

He responded with very deliberate aitches: 'Hi, Helen.'

Adam saw a movement out of the corner of his eye. Four people in robes. Adam thought of pictures of monks he had seen in books. These men didn't wear crucifixes, but there was something circular on a gold chain around each of their necks.

Suddenly Adam felt despair and wilted to the floor. No one outside the containers had hidden their faces, which made him fear he was never going to be set free. That was how it worked in films. How long would they even be kept alive?

The robed men came closer, straight to Adam's container.

'What do you want with me?' Adam demanded, standing right up close to the glass, determined not to be intimidated. 'Who the hell are you?' The other prisoners turned their backs and huddled as far away as possible. The nearest man threw back his hood and Adam looked straight into his unwavering dark eyes. He opened the hatch that the food had been sent through.

'Hello, Adam.' The voice coming through the hatch was slow, soft and relaxed on the surface, but there was also something coarse, like waves rolling over shingle. 'I've spoken to all the others and now I must speak to you. You are the most important of all of us. More important than them. More important than me.'

Adam closed his eyes and breathed out, like a parent exasperated with an annoying kid.

'My name is Bolleskine, and I'm not your opponent, but here to help you take your rightful place.'

'So you're going to get me out of here?'

Bolleskine nodded. 'Yes, of course.' He smiled as if this was obvious. 'The whole reason for your being here is so that I can free you.'

Adam frowned. *Huh?* 'That doesn't make sense.'

'I'm going to take you on a journey with me. With me and many others. You are here because you are *chosen*.'

Adam glanced at the other capsules. No one was looking his way.

'Yes,' Bolleskine continued. 'They are chosen too. Hand-picked. The very best of the generation that has not yet lost its innocence. But none of them is like you, Adam.'

'Why me?'

'Those who took you last year, when you were nearly killed, were wrong about many things, but they were not wrong about *you*. You *are* chosen. Coron and I led this group before he rebelled, like the traitor that he was. But he correctly identified you as the chosen one.'

Adam had tried to forget Coron – who had captured him the previous year, whom Adam had killed – and put that whole awful episode behind him. Coron had been evil, and also completely mad. This man was different. He was less easy to define, subtler, with an air of being other-worldly. Adam looked again into his dark eyes. For a moment he tried to capture a thought. *Yes – I have it,* Adam realized. *Coron might have suspected deep down that he was mad, but this man thinks he is completely sane.* Adam snapped back to his situation. *Get as much information as possible.*

'Where are you going to take us?'

'To the Golden Planet, where we will be free of the demons of this world. A place where there are no . . .' He paused, and Adam could see himself reflected in his eyes. 'Where there are no *bats.*'

The word made Adam wince. The comment didn't make sense – Adam hated bats and sometimes had nightmares about them, but hadn't seen any here. He peered around the cave. Maybe there were some hiding up there, clinging to the rocks. He shivered.

'You see, Adam,' Bolleskine continued, 'we have

discovered a way to see the demons that are around us.'

Adam looked contemptuously at the man. 'And when do we leave for this planet of yours?'

'Soon, now that you are with us. In a few days everyone will be gathering here.' Bolleskine smiled. 'Thank you for joining us.'

'Let me go,' said Adam. 'If I'm so important, I command you to let me go.'

'Adam, Adam,' said Bolleskine, smiling indulgently, 'at the moment you are confused, you haven't yet seen everything. But when we arrive at our new home you will be our leader. For you are half-Valdhinian. You are born of the people who live there.'

Adam said, 'What? No,' then, 'Nutter.' He shook his head, knowing that it was impossible to argue against blind belief. He just asked one more question, the same question that Abbie had asked a few days before: 'How will we get there?'

Bolleskine grabbed handfuls of his cloak as if to tear it away. 'We will free ourselves of these bodies.'

Adam understood immediately. Some – the believers – would commit suicide, and others – like him – would be killed.

*

Adam was looking at the grate and the water that flowed underneath. It smelt stale, but now there was a new, sweeter odour and something peppery. Adam went down on his hands and knees and sniffed. There was a strange spinning sensation and –

RING-RING.

It was like the sound of an old fire engine.

Then more noise:

SIT DOWN – SIT DOWN.

The noise was coming from right inside his container.

Then Adam saw shadows moving outside. They were like black rags, with threads dangling down at the edges.

The smell grew sweeter and stronger. The pepper caught in his throat.

I'm being drugged, thought Adam, his thoughts shutting down. *This isn't real.*

He closed his eyes. *This isn't real.* He covered his face. *I'm hallucinating.*

Then all was silent apart from a tapping on the glass.

'Adam, Adam.'

Knock, knock.

'Help me, Adam, help me.'

'No,' Adam shouted, 'you're not real.'

So who was he talking to? Adam peered between his fingers.

It was an old woman, turned away from him. 'You must help me. I am so old. So old, but I can't die. So tired.'

What she was saying reminded him of a poem he had been studying at school. Adam shouted at the pale cardigan and grey hair, 'Go away!'

Please don't turn round.

'Go away!'

Please don't turn round.

When the smell was even stronger, she did turn around.

His worst fear. It always produced their worst fear.

Two thin black wings, interlaced with veins, covered her face. Adam closed his eyes. *Not real. Not real.* But she was now in the blackness of his shut eyes.

The wings opened. Bats. Hundreds of bats flapped around Adam's container.

He buried his head in his hands.

Not real.

Their wings flapped faster and faster, first making a rhythm, then the beating and whooshing made a sound like a voice:

'You must . . .'

Swish. Rush.

'You must . . .'

Frenzied flapping.

'Become empty . . .'

A madness of bats.

'Of yourself.'

You must become empty of yourself.

Most of the children were screaming now. But no one could hear them in the castle above and no one could hear them in the Scottish mountains beyond.

CHAPTER 25

THE END IS NEAR (DAYS FOLLOWING TUESDAY 16TH DECEMBER 2014)

In the cavern below Castle Dreich, Adam soon understood the pattern of the days – three meals, probably drugged – and thought he was managing to keep track of how many had passed, but was more terrified about the number of days he had remaining.

He understood how the desire to escape could slip. The boredom was already intense; with nothing to focus on except vague hopes and fears, Adam frequently had to drag his mind back from aimless wandering.

Sometimes a prisoner in one of the other containers would scream or shout, and Adam hated the outbursts. Now he saw something terrible: the girl next to Helen was knocking her head against the glass wall of her container. He could see a bloody stain, and then a more distinct line of red.

'Please stop doing that to yourself,' Adam shouted. 'We need to work together.'

But the others had been there for much longer and had lost all hope.

The response was quick: almost immediately the sweet smell poured from the grate.

It was impossible to do anything when the visions came, except to retreat into the corners of your mind. This time the smell was stronger and lasted for longer. Bat after bat lay itself on Adam's head, their wings completely covering him. He could feel their thin bones and paper-like skin. They pulled tighter and tighter, pressing into his head – pressing inside his head.

His world faded away.

When Adam awoke, he was lying face down by the grate. It was frustrating to have a possible escape route so near. Frustrating and hopeless. Four screws were about an arm's length down, far beyond where his fingers could poke, at the point before the drop opened up into a much larger pipe. They were called wing-nut screws, he seemed to remember from his dad, because they had little raised wings. Even a ruler could be used to push them round, bit by bit. But he had nothing at all that could reach that far, apart from clothing, and that wouldn't work. If only he had something long and metal or wood. *If only* . . .

Adam pushed his nose against the cloak on his upper arm and could make out a fusty smell. He picked up a tissue he had been given earlier and wiped it under his arms.

Rolling it into a tube, he pushed it through the grate, watching it fall into the running water at the bottom, about four feet below, and be washed from there into a sewer pipe. *If I could get there, I could crawl through that slimy tube*, he thought. Someone had crawled through it before: the grate had certainly been bolted from underneath.

The water below was a dark and hazy blur. It ran all day and all night. But he had no idea where it went to, or where he was. One question always led to others. Did his family realize he had been kidnapped? Was he listed as a runaway? Had Megan managed to explain what was going on?

One thing is certain, Adam thought. *Whatever they do to us, I'm not going to just sit here waiting for death.*

Late one morning, Adam banged on the side of his glass prison. 'Can anyone hear me?' he called. 'Anyone?'

He looked towards Helen, putting his palms flat on the glass.

She stared back at him with blank eyes.

'I like football,' Adam said. He mimed kicking a ball. 'And cricket.' He pretended that his arm was a bat. He then lied about liking reading – well, he did like stuff that wasn't boring – and everyone understood the way to show a book.

Helen waved her fingers out to the left and right, her face full of concentration. She was a pianist, and possibly a good one.

Adam mimed his (rather poor) guitar playing, and gave a thumbs-down signal. Helen played again on her imaginary instrument and then rather coyly gave a thumbs-up.

Adam then turned round and saw a boy looking so tired his whole face seemed to sag. 'I'm Max,' he mouthed. 'Good at science – and chess.'

A younger boy, about twelve, was slowly waving, despite red, tearful eyes. Adam couldn't make out his name, but there was no mistaking his actions. He was interested in swimming, and certainly looked like an athlete. The swimmer unenthusiastically gave a double thumbs-up, presumably to show that he was once keen, but it was obvious he didn't really care any more. He pointed at himself and held up his index finger. One. Number one. The best.

Helen started pointing wildly at a distant point of the chamber. She looked terrified.

Six people were entering. The fifty-something woman and her young assistant were there, as well as four others, including Bolleskine.

The adults stood with the formality of strict teachers, apart from Bolleskine. He seemed relaxed, as if nothing mattered much. 'There will be no more communication,' he said, the hatch open so that Adam could hear, though the words were still a little dull and distant. 'Here we must become one entity, not fight to be individuals. We must empty ourselves and become one organism.' He looked at Adam. 'You are a leader, of course. But it is only after our journey that you will have your authority and become the head of our body.'

One of the men, balding and middle-aged, nondescript-looking, was carrying a small pot, about one-fifth of the size of a Coke can. Bolleskine turned to him. 'Now, before lunch, I think they need more medicine.' He turned back to Adam. 'It shows us what an evil world we live in. And why we need to leave it behind. Once we are gone, and free, it will discipline those who mocked us.'

'What?!' Adam shouted. 'What are you talking about?'

Bolleskine paused. 'The capitals of England and Scotland will see what an evil, demon-infested world we live in.' He seemed to think that Adam would be impressed.

'Adam, we have enough of our medicine to punish our capital cities. Those who have spoken against us, driven us here through wicked laws, lived disobedient lives – they will be chastised.'

Chastised means *drugged*, Adam realized. But how could you drug a whole city?

Bolleskine nodded towards the man with the container, who knelt down and pulled up a manhole cover. He tipped the dusty contents of the tub into the pipes that linked the glass prisons.

For a second Adam caught the girl's eye. He had a thought – and tried to get her to understand – but then all logic was swept from him as the sweet smell started again, but much stronger, like fly spray.

Adam pulled off his cloak and tried to stop the air coming in through the grate, but it was too late. This time the bats were closer, inside the container: next to him, crawling over him.

And there was something else behind the beating wings of the bats: the voice of a man, a measured and calm voice, teasing him again and again. *You must become empty of yourself*, it said.

CHAPTER 26

INTO THE CAVERN (FRIDAY 19TH AND SATURDAY 20TH DECEMBER 2014)

EDINBURGH

Every few seconds, somewhere in Edinburgh, someone turns on a tap and fresh water pours out, into glasses, into kettles or on to hands; other water flows into showers, washing machines and dishwashers. More than 350 million pints of water are used by the city every day.

Much of that water starts in the Megget Reservoir, far to the south of the city. Fresh water gurgles and bubbles as it is pumped north.

But no one drinks the water until it has passed through the Glencorse Water Treatment Works in the Pentland Hills. It is a modern, sophisticated operation, hidden under oak trees and covered in grass.

From there, water is carried into the city and channelled to buildings through a complicated network of pipes.

Near to the Glencorse Water Treatment Works there is a farm, and on that farm there is an old barn, and in that barn there was a rusty tractor and containers filled with the yellow crumbly drug. Hidden nearby was a pile of empty paint pots.

Standing in front of the containers was Abbie's father, Mark.

He knew that dropping the drug into the water supply would do to Edinburgh what the same material had done at Castle Dreich. He wanted to punish people for their disobedience and opposition.

LONDON

In the centre of London, near to the British Museum, deep underground, there is an old storage room. It is in a station right at the heart of one of the world's largest and busiest underground railway systems. Four million people use the London Underground every day.

The site had been selected because it was exactly in the middle of the tube network. Bolleskine knew that a gas released from there would spread throughout the entire system.

Alistair had recently returned to London from Castle Dreich. He added two more paint-pot-sized containers to his collection. He also pulled from out of his rucksack another part of the device he would use to convert the crumbly yellow drug into gas.

He knew that sending the gas into the London

Underground tunnels would set demons loose across London. He wanted to punish people for their disobedience and opposition.

CASTLE DREICH

Darkness had just fallen on Friday 19th December when the guests started to arrive.

'Welcome to Castle Dreich,' said Bolleskine, as more visitors came in through the large wooden front door. 'I'm so excited that we're all together at last.'

The castle was full of people and noise. The convention had gathered together members of the cult from across the country. There were committed members from cities and towns across Britain, but the most dedicated lived in Castle Dreich itself.

Nearly one hundred people were now in the castle. Cars and minibuses, marshalled by smiling attendants, were parked in organized lines outside. Dormitories had been set up around the castle and every room was full. Abbie had to share with a girl who had come from Newcastle.

An elderly couple looked up at the grand entrance hall to the castle. 'Isn't it exciting to be here?' said the husband. 'Not nearly as exciting as it is to meet Mr Bolleskine,' said his wife, her eyes glowing with the prospect of meeting their hero in person.

First thing in the morning, even before breakfast, everyone assembled together in the Great Hall, and Bolleskine addressed them from the raised platform at the front. 'Welcome to Castle Dreich! Welcome to you all. This is the biggest convention we have ever held – almost all our family is here.' He raised his arms to remind everyone of the size of the crowd. 'We are here for an exciting reason: the end is near.'

Almost everyone nodded and muttered in approval.

'The time for our collection is imminent,' announced Bolleskine. 'We will be taken from this place and will start a new life on our Golden Planet. If you have *worries* – you can *stop* worrying. If you have *hopes* – you can be prepared. Things are going to happen – and they are going to happen to YOU!'

There was applause and excited smiling.

'This many people cannot be wrong,' he continued, looking around the gathering. 'And I can tell you now,' he went on, in a voice so quiet they had to strain to hear, 'those of us who have been living in this castle have seen the evil that is in this world. We have seen the demons. It is those demons who stop us reaching our full potential.'

People nodded. They believed him.

Suddenly Bolleskine was louder, his hands jabbing the air. 'But some of us, I can tell you now, have also seen the Valdhinians. I spoke with them this morning. This is our time! And *you* are the people!'

This was what his audience had come to hear. They believed that the Valdhinians existed; they hoped to see them too.

Bolleskine shouted, 'I *know* that great things will happen *very* soon. Everything will be revealed to us. The end is very near!'

There was spontaneous applause and some cheering.

Abbie looked at the people around her, feeling conspicuous and lonely in her disbelief. She wondered if any others had doubts at all. But she couldn't take unnecessary risks now that she had the confidence of Bolleskine, Vee and the others.

Vee spoke gently in Abbie's ear. 'Abbie, my dear, let us go to the kitchen and prepare breakfast for those in the cavern.' Vee wanted theirs to be a mother–daughter relationship.

But Abbie didn't want a replacement mother. She remembered her dead mum and was filled with emotional determination. 'Of course,' she whispered.

Abbie's mind remained elsewhere. She thought back to what she had seen in the cavern: the arrival of the boy at the centre, the one they called Adam. She remembered the look on his face before the drug affected him. Adam had looked at her – very definitely at her. He had looked at the manhole that the drug had been put down. Then he had looked across the cavern floor to the grate in the middle of his glass container. Finally his eyes traced across the floor in the same direction that the water flowed.

Abbie – down the manhole cover – to the grate – and out with the water.

There was something about Adam's sense of purpose that made Abbie think they could work together. And if anything was going to mess up the plans of this crazy group, it would be the escape of the boy at the middle of the X.

After preparing the breakfast, Abbie returned briefly to her room. She wanted to change into the loosest clothes that she had and put on trainers.

Sitting on the temporary mattress across the room was an older girl. She was very pale with glasses, and shy. 'I'm sure you have a lot to do in the service of Bolleskine and the good people here,' she mumbled.

A wave of sadness came over Abbie – something not produced by the drug. She looked at the older girl: peculiar and lonely, probably, but not evil.

From careful eavesdropping and from her time with Vee, Abbie now knew the broad outline of everything that was intended. The poisoning of Edinburgh by her father, of London by Alistair, and the mass suicide of everyone at Castle Dreich. The capital cities that had opposed the group would be punished.

'I'll make sure everything turns out OK for you,' said Abbie.

'Thank you, you're so sweet,' said the other girl, adjusting her glasses nervously.

Abbie found it much easier to move around the castle now that there were so many other people around. She could hear talking behind doors and there were sometimes people in the corridors.

'Going somewhere, Abbie, my dear?' It was Vee.

'Yes,' said Abbie, delivering her prepared lie. 'Melissa, the girl in my room, wanted one of the handouts that we were given yesterday. I said I'd pick one up.' Abbie smiled. 'I'll be straight back.'

'OK. I'm so pleased that everything is working out now.' But Vee waited for Abbie's return – and just over five minutes later realized something was wrong. She contacted Bolleskine.

Abbie went straight towards the caverns. Every delay, every person who saw her, was a chance for her plan to go wrong. It was a long way, taking about five minutes, involving going through three doors with code pads, through cellars and along a tunnel. The old entrance from the surface, Vee said, had been closed a year or two ago – dynamited shut.

Abbie keyed in the code on the first door at the bottom of the main stairway on the ground floor: 2436. She had seen it inputted many times. This was several floors below Bolleskine's rooms, but in the same part of the castle.

One man passed her. 'Hello? Abbie?' he said, definitely questioning, though Abbie was often in this part of the castle taking food to those in the containers.

'Hi, I'm just going to see Bolleskine. He's a sort of dad to me while mine's away.' Before the conversation could proceed any further, she breezed on, turning right, as if going up towards Bolleskine's rooms.

A minute later she doubled back, down towards the cellars.

9602.

This time her nerves seemed to delay the green light, and Abbie held her breath until the door clicked open.

There were three separate cellars which had been turned into clean and organized storage rooms. On her way through, Abbie reached into a box marked 'torches' and pulled out a Petzl head torch – then, after two paces, turned around and picked up another. A hunch. After quickly testing both, she pushed them into her pocket and looked ahead to a long underground tunnel, wide enough for three to walk abreast. Modern lighting had been installed above large ventilation pipes and other wires. At the far end, about sixty yards away, was one more door with a keypad.

She waited outside the door and pulled from her pocket a small knife she had taken from the kitchen. There were a number of wires running along the tunnel, but it was the smallest black one that she was interested in. She sliced through it with her knife. The lights didn't even flicker. She hoped she had the right one.

There was no turning back now.

She had never quite been able to see this code. It

certainly had a 5 and a 3 in the middle, and she thought it started with an 8. But the last digit? It wasn't one on the right hand side of the keypad. Maybe a 4?

She quickened her pace a bit.

8 . . .

5 . . .

3 . . .

Her finger paused over the 4. Then, a guess, pressed . . . 7.

Buzz; click. The door opened.

What lay beyond was the biggest challenge of all. There was a sort of control room. Video screens showing pictures of the thirteen containers flickered on desks. Sometimes there were four people here, usually at least three. Abbie was relieved to see that today there were only two: Noah, and a man called Frank. He was a technical whizz and responsible for much of the electronics, ventilation and video surveillance.

'Hello, Abbie,' said Noah as he stood up. His eyes widened and he felt a bit nervous. He thought that Abbie was achingly pretty and wanted to marry her when they reached the new planet. Bolleskine had said that everyone would have a family.

'Hi, Noah. Hello, Frank.' Abbie turned to the older

man. 'I've been sent down by Bolleskine – you know what it's like with all the family here.' She was careful to use the right words. 'All the brothers and sisters.'

Frank leaned forward, interested to know why Abbie had arrived.

'Apparently there's a problem with the internal telephone.'

Frank immediately picked up his phone, tapped and clicked it.

'He says the wire is frayed where it feeds into the main building,' lied Abbie.

Frank frowned and tutted. 'That would affect things down here, I suppose, depending where the disconnect is . . .'

'He sent me down to ask you to get up to the castle immediately. He said that he must have contact with the cavern.'

An apparent instruction from Bolleskine brought Frank to his feet and, although he was wary, he left immediately.

Abbie knew that she had little time. As she feared, Vee had just alerted Bolleskine.

Abbie turned to Noah. 'Noah, now I'm here, I have to speak to you.' She moved closer, her blue eyes wide and innocent. 'Have you wondered how mad this all is?'

'Yes,' said Noah, looking at her mouth. He was fascinated by her tongue, lips and teeth glistening together. 'But all will be well when we arrive on the Golden Planet.'

Abbie knew that time was running out. 'No – I mean now, doing all of this. Keeping people down here.'

'But . . . Abbie, you know that this is necessary.'

Abbie's smile hid a fountain of desperate frustration. She was never going to win Noah round; it was going to have to be Plan B. 'Noah, when we're on the Golden Planet, I want us to be together.'

Noah smiled. 'Oh, Abbie . . . That's wonderful. So do I.' It was all so sudden to Noah – sudden and *real*, though he had imagined this many times.

Abbie put a hand on his shoulder. 'Everything will be perfect there. Can you imagine it?' Noah smiled pleasantly and closed his eyes for a second.

In that instant, Abbie pushed her right hand up and against Noah's chin. Then she put one hand over his mouth and, vice-like, grabbed the back of his head with the other. She forced about half-an-inch square of crumbly yellow drug, taken from the kitchen store, into his mouth.

Noah's eyes were full of surprise as he fell to the ground. It was a large dosage, not quite enough to cause permanent damage, but Abbie had to be sure she could incapacitate him.

'I'm sorry,' she muttered.

She went back to the door, opened it and swung a metal chair at the keypad on the castle side, buckling and smashing it. The door clicked shut and she pulled across the bolts on the cavern side.

Noah writhed on the ground in tormented agony, tearing at his face, aware of nothing other than his own fears.

Frank was obediently testing one of the phones in the castle when Bolleskine and Vee passed, with three other people. They were running towards the cavern.

CHAPTER 27

SOMETHING IN THE PIPELINE (SATURDAY 20TH DECEMBER 2014)

Bolleskine headed the group that ran down the white-walled tunnel towards the cavern. He could see that the crumpled keypad was hanging loose.

'Abbie? Abbie!' he shouted into the metal door. 'Let me in!' He listened but couldn't hear anything other than the hum of ventilation and the faintest trickle of water. 'Abbie! *Abbie!*' He pounded on the secure door. Lips tight with anger, he turned to Frank, who had followed, annoyed and embarrassed at having been tricked by Abbie. 'We must open this.'

'It's an electromagnetic lock. We need to turn the power off.'

'It's controlled from the other side. Just cut the power to here – rip out the fuse, snap the connection, whatever it takes.' Bolleskine forced his shoulder against the door but it barely made an impact.

Frank ran off towards the main fuse box.

Abbie raced over to the glass containers. 'I'm going to do what I can to get you out,' she called.

Adam waved frantically with one hand, slamming the other on the glass. 'Thank you,' he mouthed, as Abbie came closer. 'Can you undo these bolts?' He pointed at the fixings on the outside of the containers.

Abbie stood less than a pace away from him, separated by the thick glass. Some of the drug still coursed through her, but weak enough that she was able to ignore the spiders she imagined scuttling about the cavern. 'No.' She shook her head in case Adam couldn't hear.

'There's no way you can smash the glass,' said Adam with extravagant gestures and a look of wild despair, his words unheard by Abbie, but understood.

'No,' Abbie shouted again, impatient, opening the hatch so that Adam could hear.

His words escaped in a rush: 'In that case, you'll have to go down and under and—'

'Yes,' shouted Abbie, running to the nearest manhole cover. 'I know.'

'Then what?' screamed Adam.

'I don't know. Shut up!' she bellowed back.

Just as Abbie reached the cover to go underground, all the lights went out. It wasn't the darkness of a cinema, with emergency lighting, nor the darkness of night, with light from the moon and stars; this was the utter darkness of being underground, as dark with your eyes open as with them closed.

'Use your mobile phones as torches,' ordered Bolleskine. 'We still have to force the bolts.'

The door gave slightly as they pushed and kicked at it.

Frank arrived with a crowbar and torches, relieved that the stores were nearby in the cellar, and that the castle was equipped for all possible difficulties.

Bolleskine almost immediately wedged the sharp end of the crowbar in by the lock and managed to force the door open a fraction more. There was the sound of rending metal and a loud crack as one of the locks snapped. The bottom half of the door was now about two inches ajar.

'It's the bolt at the top we need to force,' said Frank.

Bolleskine gave him a withering look, then kicked the door twice and pushed three times with his shoulder.

On the third heave the door opened and dancing torchlight spilt into the cavern, intermittently shining on Noah, who still clawed at his own face, whimpering in mad terror.

'Get the lights back on,' said Bolleskine. 'Quickly! If she's done anything to Adam, I'll kill her with my bare hands.'

*

Adam sensed bats flying around – but these drug-induced creatures didn't have to obey ordinary laws of flight; they could pass through the glass of his container and they stayed near him, their fine veiny wings flapping, their tiny sharp mouths squeaking, when he tried to push them away.

Abbie was on her knees in the pipe, sliding the cover back on top of her. Her head torch cast light down the tube. Water swelled past her: it wasn't very deep, nor especially fast, but it came about one-quarter of the way up a pipe that had a diameter of just over eighteen inches – big enough to crawl through, but still claustrophobically small. And the smell was beginning to rise – a mix of urine, bleach, and stale dampness. She looked up and saw a spider completely blocking her path. 'I wish I was scared of kittens,' she muttered, and forced herself to crawl down the tube towards it, slipping and banging her head, but going in a straight line towards Adam's container.

'I'm here – I'm here,' called Adam, bending close to the grate, trying to direct her in the darkness, unsure of how the pipes were connected. First he saw flickering light, then the pipe below was properly lit, and then Abbie's damp blonde hair appeared.

'This pipe stinks,' she said.

'If you undo those four screws, we can lift the fixing up.' Adam pointed.

'Keep quiet,' said Abbie, twisting one of the screws with clumsy cold fingers. 'If you were so clever, you wouldn't be stuck in a box.' The screw came undone and she started twisting the second.

It was during the undoing of the third that Adam said: 'Thanks. I'm Adam by the way.'

The third wing-nut dropped off. One to go.

Abbie didn't stop. 'I'm Abbie, and for me it's spiders.'

'Bats,' said Adam. 'Hurry up!' He could see flickering light at the corner of the cavern.

The grate came loose. Adam pulled it up and sat on the edge, about to lower himself down, when he saw a torch coming closer, and quickly.

Adam took off his cloak, and in shorts and T-shirt slid down the hole that had teased and tormented him, and his bare feet plunged into water. Then, slightly crouching and hemmed in by the narrow pipe, he pulled the grate neatly back into position from underneath.

Bolleskine arrived and shone his torch into Adam's container. 'What?!' he roared. Frantic, he shone his torch towards the other twelve prisoners.

They put their arms up to shield themselves from

the beam just as the main lights came back on. Before, the cavern lights had seemed a dim glow, but suddenly they felt piercingly bright. They confirmed that Adam's container was completely empty. Everyone stared in a moment of stunned silence. Hope stirred in the captured children; anger stormed through Bolleskine.

'What?!' It was the same booming shout as before. Bolleskine turned to Frank and the others. 'He must have . . .'

They all peered at the floor. Frank pointed to the manhole cover.

Bolleskine nodded. 'They can't get away without passing this point.' A tiny smile. 'Open it up. When they pass by, we'll drag them out.'

As Adam and Abbie splashed through the pipe on hands and knees, they had to pass under three other glass prisons. Adam peered up at the square of light less than a yard above him, frustrated that they couldn't risk saving anyone else. His left shoulder gave the occasional twinge, but he ignored it.

Abbie still had both torches, so Adam squirmed after her in near darkness, unspeaking. The pipes were not only used to administer the drug, they were also used for the removal of human waste from twelve people, so Adam didn't like to think of what foulness he was putting his hands and legs in. He squelched on.

Above them, Bolleskine and the others waited for Adam and Abbie to get to the point where they would pass under the manhole cover.

Adam and Abbie moved on, cold, excited, driven by the lure of escape.

Bolleskine and the others waited, increasingly doubtful. 'What if they've gone down *with* the water, away from the entrance?' Bolleskine asked.

Frank shrugged. 'They'd follow the old river into the caves. But that would be mad, completely stupid – they'd be trapped.'

'We cannot leave without Adam.' Bolleskine breathed out deeply. 'Though fate will bring him back to us.'

Following the water slightly downhill, Adam and Abbie passed under the last grating and then came to the point where another pipe joined theirs. The water was deeper here, nearly halfway up the sides, and flowing faster. Then the pipe went steadily downhill, and they both started slipping, having to push out with both arms and force their back and knees against the pipe to prevent themselves being washed away.

Abbie stopped. 'Being in here is really getting to me. We're going to drown.'

'We can't go back,' said Adam.

'Listen,' Abbie said, gritting her teeth to keep herself together, 'I can see ahead. This pipe gets even steeper.'

'Even if I could go back, I'm not going to,' Adam hissed.

At that moment Abbie slipped. There were knocks and scrapes and swear words, then silence.

Adam was completely alone in the darkness, deep beneath a wintry Scottish mountain, pursued by maniacs, following a girl he didn't know. Just as he was debating whether to go forward or back, he felt himself slide.

Bolleskine looked intently at two of his most loyal men. 'I can't follow them; I have one hundred people in the castle. This is the most important moment in our history. We will have no delay; we will all travel tonight.' He gave a flicker of a smile. 'You two will have to go after him. The quickest way is down the pipe – otherwise we need to drill and blast away this concrete.'

'We'll bring him back,' said one of the men.

'Make it so,' Bolleskine said. 'We continue as planned.'

CHAPTER 28

THE CAVES
(SATURDAY 20TH DECEMBER 2014)

Adam splashed into icy water and felt his hands press against sharp rocks. He spluttered and swallowed water; bubbles rose past him in a flurry. Then he felt himself being heaved up and backwards. He staggered to his feet and was dazzled as he found himself looking into Abbie's headlamp. 'Where are we?' he said, shivering slightly.

Abbie handed him a torch and shone hers around the cave they were in. It was a jagged oval shape, about a quarter of the size of a football pitch and at least twenty feet high, thirty in places. They were standing knee-deep in water that covered most of the floor, apart from two or three boulders. Stalactites pointed down at them from above. To the left there was scree, the rubble formed over the years by crumbling rocks. Abbie followed it upward with her torch and at the top spotted a rope strung between rusty iron rods. Then they saw a neater tunnel carved into the side.

'They used to mine here,' said Abbie. 'Lead and gold, according to . . .' she paused. 'According to my dad.'

Adam sensed that this was not something to ask about now. 'Can we get out?' he asked. 'Or will we just go deeper and deeper into the mountain until we get lost and end up looking like Gollum?'

'We're going to find out. Let's go.' Abbie set off towards the bank of rubble that would take them to the tunnel. 'And ignore the spider that's over there.' She pointed to the left above the pipe.

Adam looked. He saw a huge bat instead. 'Are you scared of bats?'

'Don't be silly,' she said. 'They're sweet.'

'Like spiders.'

Climbing the rocks was difficult in places, but they pushed and heaved one another calmly, until suddenly a new noise echoed through the cave, emanating from the pipe.

Their eyes meeting in silent resolve, they scrambled up the last few feet. Just as they were about to head further into the mountain through the tunnel, there was a dull roar and a man arrived with a splash in the pool. He got to his feet, holding his head and pointing his torch at the blood on his hands. Suddenly he turned off his torch, and the second that Abbie's and Adam's remained lit was enough to allow him to see them. 'Adam, Abbie – stop!' he shouted. 'You don't understand what you're missing out on.' He started towards them just as there was another garbled roar and someone else was spat out of the bottom of the pipe.

Adam and Abbie ran into the tunnel, keeping low and having to crouch right down in places. The tunnel wasn't quite straight: it twisted slightly, and sometimes there were recesses off it, so it was difficult to know how far they had gone.

Before long, not surprisingly, Adam hit his head. He was knocked off his feet and ended up sitting down, lucky not to have damaged his head torch. He could feel a bump, but thought there was no blood. Abbie immediately came back and shone her torch down as Adam waggled his head from side to side as if trying to shake off pain. 'There should be a *Mind Your Head* sign,' he whispered.

Abbie didn't seem to do sympathy. 'Don't hit your head again. Ready?'

Immediately afterwards, the tunnel split in two. The man-made route veered left, and what looked like an entrance to a natural cave went to the right.

Abbie turned to Adam. 'I say that way,' she muttered, pointing left.

'No – right,' said Adam, indicating the rougher route.

'Why? We could get trapped.'

Adam looked at Abbie's head. 'Can you see something to your right, down that passage?'

'One of those *things*,' Abbie mumbled. She didn't want to say the word *spider*.

'Me too, but I see a bat. With big wings and dripping fangs.' Adam tingled with fright. 'And we're going to both run straight through the bastard creatures. Come on,' he said, pulling her by the hand.

'I'm going to punch you when this is all over,' said Abbie, turning right, stepping over rocks, dipping under outcrops and running through the legs of a huge, drug-induced spider.

When the men reached the same dividing point, Adam and Abbie had gone far enough ahead for them to be unsure which fork to follow. They split. One went left down the man-made tunnel. The other went right, following Adam and Abbie, his torch shining on scattered items discarded over the years: planks of wood, rusty lamps, a bucket with a hole in the bottom – the remnants of a working mine.

The tunnel had narrowed as Abbie had warned it might, but occasionally there were alcoves jutting off, so the pair paused opposite one another at a place that had hiding places.

Footsteps echoed behind them.

'I'm tired of running away,' Abbie said, holding a cast-off pickaxe handle she had found. 'You can look away if you like.'

Adam looked around for a weapon of his own.

The man blundered along the passage, torchlight announcing his approach, unaware that the pair hid in the darkness, armed and waiting.

It was Adam who struck first. With all of his strength, he whacked his plank into their pursuer's stomach, then – as the man bent over in sudden pain – he brought it down on the back of his head. The man made a small attempt to put one hand to his wound, then let out an anguished groan, and lay still.

'You can look away if you like,' said Adam grimly.

Abbie struck the prostrate man with her pickaxe handle. 'We're taking no chances.'

Down the other tunnel, the second man heard the noise of a struggle. Echoes made his colleague's groan sound as loud as an elephant's trumpet. The man reversed and, unbeknown to Adam and Abbie, darted back down the other tunnel after them.

Adam and Abbie carried on through the mountain: at times the passageway was so narrow they had to squeeze sideways; then the ceiling dropped much lower, though luckily in a part where it was as wide as at the start. They crept on until rock came down and scree rose up, leaving a tiny gap between – maybe only twelve inches high in places.

'Adam! Abbie! You will not do this to ME!' The shout was not far away.

'I know that voice,' said Abbie. She described the man in two rude words. 'We don't want to face him.'

'Ladies first,' said Adam, pointing his torch beam at the narrow gap and brandishing his plank like a swordfighter.

'Coward,' replied Abbie.

The second that Abbie's feet disappeared through the gap, Adam followed.

The opening was jagged both above and below: clothes, and then skin, were scraped and torn. Adam followed close behind Abbie. All they could do was wriggle along, teeth-like stones digging into them both above and below. The only good thing was that it was wide despite being low. It was as they reached its very tightest point – where the clearance was barely more than nine inches – that Adam saw their route lit by a bobbing torch approaching from behind.

'Hurry up,' he urged through gritted teeth.

'It's a bit higher here,' Abbie said. *A bit higher* meant fifteen inches.

Adam felt something tugging on his lower leg. He kicked out violently, perhaps hitting rock, perhaps hitting the man. Whichever, as the passage opened slightly and they moved faster, Adam could hear his pursuer struggling to squeeze his fully grown adult form through the gap.

Adam then heard Abbie screech and shout something, but couldn't make out what. A few seconds later, he too emerged and found himself in a much larger cave. Abbie at reached the bottom of a forty-five-degree slide of scree about three or four times her height. She was shining her torch into a deep pool of clear water that blocked their exit.

Adam twisted himself around so that he scrambled down the rocks on his feet, looking at the pool as he descended. 'He's not far behind,' he gabbled. 'It looks deep. Wait a second.'

Without a pause, adrenalin coursing through him, he advanced two paces from the bottom of the rock pile, stuck his hands out ahead of him – took a deep breath – and dived into the icy water.

The pool was certainly deep, and Adam could see immediately that it was long as well, extending far beyond the rock at the end of the cave. *I'll do ten strokes out*, he thought, *I'll have to see if it leads anywhere*, but without any idea what he was heading into or how far he'd be able to hold his breath. The cold bit into him. He counted his strokes, forcing himself on.

After ten it was clear that the channel was narrowing rather than widening, and Adam's lungs were almost bursting. Then he thought he could see the surface.

Push on.

Five more strokes.

Push on.

Two more – lungs hurting.

I won't be able to get back.

Kick. Heave.

And Adam's head burst above water. He didn't have to shine his torch far to see his surroundings. An almost circular and vertical shaft stretched far above him, probably scalable with ropes and crampons, but not by two soaking-wet teenagers.

He'd got his breath back and was about to return to where he had left Abbie, when her head bobbed up, blinking and shaking water off her hair. They both had to tread water.

'I was about to come back. How did you know I'd

found somewhere?' Adam asked.

'You didn't come back.' Her voice echoed up the shaft.

'I could have drowned.'

'Yeah. I did wonder about that.'

They knew they couldn't stay where they were.

'You swim like an eel,' Abbie said. 'Get down there again and see if the tunnel continues on the other side.'

An eel? Adam thought that was probably a compliment.

He ducked back under. But this time it was far more complicated. There were more rocks – it was confusing, more enclosed, and harder to see, though the torch was so far living up to its waterproof claim. Eventually he had to push himself backwards and return to Abbie unsuccessful.

'Wait here,' he gasped. 'I just needed air. I'll be quick.' He was gone again.

Adam went left this time at each junction: left, left, left, and then, far ahead, down a long tunnel that went slightly uphill and narrowed, he could see the surface of the water.

Rising for a quick intake of air, he could see a much larger cavern, with rocks to climb on to. But when he tried to return, he realized that the rocks and channels all looked the same: he had to concentrate on going right, right, right as the distressing and tight breathless feeling in his chest grew.

Once more he gasped as he surfaced next to Abbie.

'I've found another cavern. Trust me,' he said.

Abbie looked him in the eye. 'I don't *do* trust.'

Their head torches filled the small cavern with sparkling light. 'You *could* stay here.'

He sank under and Abbie followed. But as Adam glanced behind he could see another torch approaching from the first underwater channel.

Adam swam left, left, left, and saw Abbie still behind him. All of the tunnels were completely filled with water – no chance of a breath. The final long stretch towards the surface was very narrow, and towards the end there was a protruding rock which left a small gap that could only be passed with hands ahead or tight to body. Adam had slipped through without difficulty, but Abbie, slightly larger and less of a natural in the water, couldn't pass as easily.

Adam looked ahead at what he was sure was the surface – and back to Abbie's wide-eyed panic. She was shaking her head, lips tight, eyes desperate.

Adam was also running out of oxygen fast, his lungs screaming for a breath that would only bring in water.

He went back to Abbie and reached out his hands. Behind her, he could see a torch beam wiggling closer.

She made a huge effort to stretch her arms through . . .

Their hands met.

Adam pulled her through.

Then they wildly clawed up to the surface.

Both coughed and heaved as they emerged into yet another cave and crawled out of the water on to damp stones.

'He's catching us up,' spluttered Adam.

Abbie picked up a rock. 'If he makes it through and his head comes out of this water, I'm going to smash it in.'

Adam directed his torch beam round their latest stopping point. It was a large and beautiful cave, easily large enough to stand up in; stalactites hung down like organ pipes and damp rocks welled up like bubbling lava.

At exactly the same time, Adam and Abbie noticed different things.

Adam held up a small plastic strip from the back of a plaster, which he'd picked off the rock by his foot. 'Someone has been here before. There must be a way out . . .'

Abbie wasn't listening. She was looking at an arm rising towards them through the water. As Adam fell silent and watched, she grimaced, took aim and lifted her rock to shoulder height.

CHAPTER 29

THE CHIMNEY
(SATURDAY 20TH DECEMBER 2014)

The man was dead. His arm floated loosely ahead of him as if in surrender. He bobbed face down in the water for thirty seconds or more while Adam and Abbie stared. He must have had trouble getting through the same gap that had nearly beaten Abbie.

Strangely, they were both more unsettled by the arrival of a dead body than they would have been by a living opponent. It made them realize just what a deadly gamble with drowning their escape had been.

Abbie nudged the man's body with her foot and he slowly rolled over. 'I knew him back at the castle – one of Bolleskine's favourites.' For a short while they saw his open mouth and eyes glassily looking upward, then he was face down again.

'It's better this way,' said Adam. 'Otherwise we would have had to hurt him.'

'Yeah.' Abbie turned to Adam. 'Let's get out of here. If we can.'

'We can talk over there.' Adam didn't mention wanting

to get away from the body. He clambered over rocks to the other side of the cavern, pointing his torch at the intricate natural designs around him as he did so. Abbie followed.

Both of them then focused their torches on the tiny strip that Adam had found. It certainly did look like the thin plastic layer that is taken off the back of a plaster. In any case, it was man-made. 'There *must* be a way out. This is *proof* that someone else has been in here,' said Adam.

Abbie stood up and shone her torch around the cave. 'There's something up there,' she said, her beam resting on a mouth-like opening at the top of a pile of boulders.

Shivering, they explored. They found themselves in a tunnel that went horizontally for about fifteen feet, then doubled back at a tight angle into a long forty-five-degree shaft rising up between two slightly different types of rock.

When it started to rise, Abbie looked for a handhold.

'It'll be like climbing up a chimney,' Adam said, peering above him.

'More like crawling up a huge arse,' said Abbie grimly. 'It smells disgusting.'

It was difficult to climb: sometimes smooth and slippery, sometimes jagged, but Adam found himself remembering what it's possible to do when there's absolutely no other choice. Abbie swore at the rocks and occasionally at Adam, but she never stopped climbing. She was as tough as any boy Adam knew.

He had never dealt with anyone quite like her before. Megan was Adam's measure for all girls – other girls were just a percentage as good as she was. Abbie didn't seem to be on the same scale at all. She was one-hundred-per-cent Abbie.

As they climbed, Abbie prepared Adam for the likelihood that they were not going to be able to do anything to prevent Bolleskine's hideous plan. She knew the full outline and some details of it and spoke while climbing. 'I'm certain that people at the castle are going to commit suicide,' she said, heaving herself up. 'A mass event.' She paused. 'Some of them won't even need persuading. They believe they're going to be transported to another planet, and you lot in capsules were their oh-so-talented super-leaders.'

Adam laughed bitterly. He wished for the thousandth time that he was a normal kid.

'Yes. What a bunch of loons.' She looked down at Adam, her feet against one rock, her back wedged against another. 'What was your special talent?'

Adam raised his eyebrows. 'Now *that*'d be telling,' he

said. He was getting to like Abbie.

She rolled her eyes. 'Whatever! Listen – that drug is going to be spread through Edinburgh and London. We need to think about how to stop it.' She stopped climbing again. 'Adam . . .' It was the first time she had actually used his name. 'There's another reason why I need your help. Of all people, my stupid dad is the one who's going to be putting that stuff into Edinburgh's water; he's gone mad with grief after my mum died earlier this year and I can't get through to him to convince him what he's doing is wrong. But I have to stop him. I can't lose him as well as Mum.'

Adam only said, 'No.' But sympathy was etched on his face.

'And we're finished.' She had stepped out on to a ledge and was looking in dismay at a smooth section about eight feet high at the bottom of a tall, nearly vertical, funnel. It was like being inside an old-fashioned factory chimney.

'Wait!' said Adam. 'Turn off your torch.' High above them there was the faintest hint of daylight. 'And feel.' There was a very slight breeze.

'Great. We're still dead.' Abbie looked at the walls above. After the smooth section, they were uneven but almost sheer, stretching up and up, dangerously high.

'Unless we could somehow get to there –' she directed her torch's beam to the start of the rougher section – 'then there, and there –' rough ledges higher up were lit – 'and to there.' At the very top there seemed to be an exit, where light was seeping in.

'Let's go,' they both said at the same time.

The problem was that although either one of them could be heaved up past the smooth section to the point where it would be possible to climb from, but the other would be left behind. But Adam had a plan.

First Abbie climbed up on Adam's shoulders, her dripping wet jumper dangling from her ankle, double-knotted. 'Stand still,' she shouted as she wobbled, moving one foot and then the other on to a narrow shelf high above Adam, wedging them tight into the crevice.

Adam tugged on her jumper.

'Hold on,' shouted Abbie. 'You'll drag me down, numbskull.' She tried different handholds and angled herself firmly behind an overhang. 'Now try.'

She held tight and Adam scrabbled up the makeshift jumper-rope. The fabric stretched, the seams widened, and then, cotton strand by cotton strand, began to rip.

Adam climbed on regardless . . .

He managed to get his left hand on Abbie's foot and

his right in a fissure, then swung his legs up – just, just, by the narrowest of tiny margins, getting his knee on to the same small ledge that Abbie was standing on. 'Help!' he croaked.

Abbie found a good crack in the rock to hold on to with her left hand, then reached down and started pulling Adam up by his top. His foot went on to the small ledge and somehow he scrambled up, partly by using Abbie's legs and then the top of her trousers, all done through ugly determination rather than precision art.

'Phew,' he said as he collapsed against the rock. 'Sorry to use you as a rope.'

'Worst excuse I've ever known for getting your hands on a girl,' Abbie said dismissively.

Adam tried to ignore her comment. But the combination of athleticism, damp hair and wet, clingy clothes made her suddenly seem very attractive. A jangle of guilt followed as he thought of Megan. 'Now we mustn't look down,' he said.

On a school trip, in a harness, they would have been wary of tackling such a climb, but a sort of autopilot took over. The ascent was helped by the fact that, higher up, the funnel was narrower, and closer to square than round. This meant they could use two sides. And having two of them, working as one unit, was essential when it came to tackling the trickiest sections.

Above them, Abbie could make out a sliver of grey sky. It made her wonder whether the drug was still strong enough for her to see a forest of spiders when she was outside. She paused, looking at something just above her head. 'Adam,' she said, 'you know, I haven't seen any spiders for a while. At least, not *obvious* ones.'

'No,' he mumbled, easing himself up past a jagged rock. 'I haven't seen any bats.' He had to stop to avoid bumping into her foot.

'Ah,' she said, very gently poking something with her finger, 'I have some bad news.' She had spotted a large colony of about fifty hibernating bats less than an arm's length above her. 'You're going to have to keep looking down.'

'I'm used to seeing them,' Adam said breezily. 'They make my skin crawl, but rather an imaginary bat than a real one.'

'Er . . .' Abbie said.

Adam glanced at her face, then took a sharp intake of breath when he saw what she was looking up at. 'Bloody hell. They *are* real ones,' he murmured. He looked down at his hands going one over the other on the rocks. He hummed something tuneless, trying to distract himself. But at the very end he couldn't stop himself looking up.

There was one bat slightly on its own away from the dangling mass. It was brown, furrier than Adam expected, and had long ears tucked gently under its wings. It hung, quiet and helpless, not like the ferocious flapping creatures of his nightmares.

He shook himself and quickly moved past. 'Nailed it.'

The exit was a small mouth on a vast hillside. It was much colder outside than in the cave. The breeze disguised a rise in temperature that was thawing the snow rapidly. Fortunately, they were both drier by now, if still damp. Adam was only wearing shorts and a T-shirt. Both were covered in scratches and bruises, and every muscle ached.

Abbie pointed to something far off to the right. 'I think that's the road that leads to the castle. I only went down it once. But that would mean the castle is behind that hill.' She waved her hand at a patchily snow-covered expanse.

'Let's make for the main road and get help,' said Adam.

'We need to be quick,' said Abbie, anxious now. 'Bolleskine wants it all to happen tonight.'

'How can you be so sure?'

Abbie explained. 'It's the new moon – when the moon doesn't reflect light and things are at their darkest. He was always going on about the new moon being the important thing, not the full moon.' She looked straight at Adam.

'So we've got, say, eleven hours or something?' he asked.

Abbie nodded glumly. 'Maths your strength, is it?'

Adam sighed.

CHAPTER 30

MEGAN
(SATURDAY 20TH DECEMBER 2014)

Adam and Abbie hurried across the hillside. The snow was wet and heavy, little more than slush in places. Adam's bare feet were mercifully numb, but they were both shivering. The sun, although low in the sky, glittered on the mountains across the valley.

Abbie was right about the castle being behind the hill. After they headed across one empty field and climbed over a neglected stone wall, there was a view of the end of the loch. They stood and looked at it for a moment, worried that they were seeing something that was also visible from the castle.

As they walked and jogged towards the main road as quickly and directly as possible, it became impossible not to be within sight of the track that approached the castle, though it was far below them. There was no shelter. 'If the helicopter comes, we're finished,' said Abbie. But it didn't.

They saw three vehicles going to the castle, and two went the other way. Each time, they dived to the ground.

Eventually they were faced with the choice of either going high over a mountain or risking the more direct and open route nearer the track, where only a very few trees and bushes bravely fought against the winter. 'No one will be looking for us out here,' said Adam. 'If anything, they'll be digging into those caves. I'm for the short cut.'

'Yeah,' said Abbie. 'But we'll have to fight if they find us. I mean a real fight again. OK?'

Only one vehicle passed in the distance. It was while they were going down a slope into a barren valley. Adam and Abbie both hid behind a final cluster of thin trees and didn't notice that it was a police Range Rover until it was too late. Despite their wild shouts and energetic waving, it drifted away from them at a steady speed and was gone. They both asked *what if* questions, all unresolved by the time they reached the end of the track.

The main road was a dual carriageway curving smoothly away through the mountains. A red articulated lorry passed in a mist of cold spray and sounded its horn as Adam and Abbie stepped up on to the verge. Lorries and cars sped past, also throwing up enough water to make other drivers use their windscreen wipers.

They stood next to a blue-and-white post with some numbers on it. 'This is meant to tell us where the nearest emergency phone is, I think,' said Adam. 'But I've no idea how it works.'

They walked on a little way, then saw a lay-by in the distance and broke into a run. More vehicles raced past. Shouts came from a couple of passing cars, but it was impossible to hear what was said.

They had no choice but to stand in the lay-by and try to flag someone down. They both waved vigorously, looking like overenthusiastic and underdressed hitchhikers. Every time a car passed without stopping, Abbie would shout abuse after it. They knew time was slipping away.

Eventually a green lorry approached with a hiss and a squeak, slowing down, and they saw that its indicator was flashing. A large Eddie Stobart trailer stopped in front of them.

Adam ran round to the driver's window. 'Can we use your phone?'

'And hello to you,' said the driver in a deep Scottish burr.

'I'm sorry, but we're desperate,' said Adam.

'Are you and the lassie in some sort of trouble?'

'Yes, you could say that.' Adam put his hands on the driver's door.

'We need to call the police,' added Abbie.

'Aye,' said the driver, slowly extracting and examining a mobile phone from the jacket on the back of his seat. 'You seem to be in very good luck. I have one wee blob of reception.' He switched his hazard lights on and leaned over to open the other door.

Sitting in the cab, Abbie sighed with relief when she heard a crackly voice at the end of the phone. There was just enough signal to make a connection. She was put through to the police.

'My name is Abbie Hopkins,' she started. 'I need to report something serious.'

There was a pause. 'Thank you.' Another much longer pause. 'Thank you, Abbie. Please hold the line.'

Abbie turned to Adam: 'I don't believe it. They're making me wait.'

'If you're one mile an hour over the speed limit, the police are keen enough,' said the lorry driver sympathetically.

After another long pause and intermittent clicks on the line, a different voice was heard. 'Hello, Abbie. Where are you?'

'On a road in the Highlands.' She looked at the sign ahead. 'I think it's the A9.'

'Abbie,' the voice was low and a bit cynical, like a disappointed teacher, 'we have spoken to your father and

233

must ask you to wait for a police officer to pick you up. Do you have a boy called Adam Grant with you?'

'No, I'm on my own.' The lie spilt out just in case it was useful later. 'I'm worried about what is going on at Castle Dreich,' she continued. 'Just send someone there to have a look.'

'We have, Abbie. Two police officers have seen the meeting and confirmed that everything is in order. They spoke with the man in charge and we have seen your father here in Edinburgh.'

'Send them again, for God's sake! My father is part of the problem.' Abbie pressed one hand to her mouth to prevent herself adding something rude.

'We know *all* about your argument, Abbie.' It was a patronizing tone. 'Where did you say you were?'

'I'm . . .' Abbie looked at Adam and out of the window, and the driver started to say something. 'Actually, I can be more precise. I'm at the water-treatment place outside Edinburgh. Can you come to get me?' She put the phone down and turned to the driver, smiling as sweetly as possible. 'Please, Mr Driver, can we just have five more minutes of your time?'

'I suppose – only five, mind.'

Abbie started to say something, but Adam was louder,

talking over her: 'Listen, listen. Stop. You don't know much about me, but trust me. The police are going to be useless, at least until they understand what's really going on. We need to split up.'

'There are *three* problems!' Abbie used her fingers as if she had to make it really simple for Adam. 'Castle Dreich –' one finger – 'Edinburgh –' two – 'and London.'

'I know, if you'll just listen. You go to your dad. That was a smart move with the cops. I'll go back to the castle and try to save the other kids.' His mind was whirring.

'And then we'll fly down to London, with no money to get us there, for this evening?' said Abbie.

The driver, half listening as he got out of the cab for a fag break, smiled indulgently.

'No. I know someone down there who can help.' Adam addressed the driver: 'Can I borrow your phone again, please?'

'Aye.' The driver handed it through the cab window, rooting out some cigarettes from his jacket at the same time.

Adam couldn't remember Megan's mobile number. He pressed his hand against his forehead and tried to visualize typing it into his contacts, tried to recall hearing it on his voice messages, but it was hopeless. The more he struggled to remember, the more it eluded him.

'It's Saturday lunchtime,' he said, dialling her home number. 'She'll be in.' He handed the phone to Abbie. 'Just ask for Megan. Say you're a friend from school.'

After three rings a man answered.

'Hello, it's Georgia here from school. Can I speak to Megan?'

Georgia? Adam mouthed.

There was a bit of chatter and a shout on the other end of the line, then Megan's voice: 'Hello? Who is it?'

Abbie handed the phone to Adam.

'It's Adam. Don't panic – don't say it's me – I'm fine – but I need your help.'

Megan thought, just for a second. 'Yes, Georgia, I'm free this afternoon,' she replied.

'You're amazing, Megan. Look, I'm still in Scotland, but I'm fine.' He wasn't going to mention the being kidnapped, imprisoned and drugged, nearly drowning, almost falling to his death side of things. 'But there's a problem and, usual story for us, the police won't help. It's all . . . complicated . . .'

'That sounds great, Georgia,' Megan parroted. 'Shall I come over to your place?'

'There's a man, he's . . .'

'Thin, with a birthmark on his left cheek, um, nasty, and he wears glasses,' said Abbie. 'Called Alistair.'

'Got that? That's Abbie, she's helping me.'

Abbie continued, 'And he's going to put poison gas into the London Underground *somehow* at the British Museum stop.'

'Oh yes,' said Megan, while her parents listened to her half of the conversation, 'I'm sure we can help one another.'

'There will be containers of a drug, and probably a large machine of some sort – a big operation. The stop for the British Museum. You need to go there and get the police or someone to stop him.'

'That's great, Georgia,' said Megan. 'Sounds useful. I'll bring my textbook.'

'Get her mobile number,' Abbie said, then shook her head, implying Adam was being dim.

A pad and pen were on the dashboard. The driver was still outside, smoking, so Abbie grabbed a sheet and wrote while Megan said her number.

'Megan, you have to go this afternoon. It'll all happen today or tonight.'

'Good, I'll see if I can come over. I didn't really get it in class either. And I know we need it for GCSE.' Megan cradled the phone in her hand for a second, then airily asked if she could go out to see Georgia so that they could do their homework together.

Megan went into her room and switched on her computer. She typed in *British Museum*, then went through to the *Getting Here* page on the museum's website.

A map came up on the screen, with the British Museum in the middle.

'Adam!' she muttered in frustration. The British Museum was almost exactly in the middle of *four* different tube stations: Tottenham Court Road, Holborn, Russell Square and Goodge Street. The first two were a *bit* closer, but it all depended which entrance you went into the museum.

'I can't go to all four,' she said to herself.

After a pause she dialled a number: Rachel. Then another: Asa. Then a third: Leo. Each time she said the same thing, more or less. 'I'm asking for a huge favour. I need you to meet me outside the British Museum, by the front gate, right by the place I was kidnapped about a year ago, in one hour.'

'Of course, Meg,' said Rachel.

'Sure,' said Leo.

'Okey-dokey,' said Asa. 'I'll get out of bed and put some clothes on. It's just as well this isn't a Skype.'

'I need to get moving,' said the driver.

Adam and Abbie were frantically discussing plans. The lorry driver had agreed to take Abbie into Edinburgh as he was going that way, and he even gave Adam some leftover sandwiches, a tatty coat and some old trainers that were lying around in his cab. The clothes smelt of smoke, but Adam had never more gratefully received a gift.

Outside the open door of the cab, Adam gave Abbie a quick hug.

'Come on,' shouted the driver.

'You know what you're doing?' said Abbie.

'If *you* know what *you're* doing,' said Adam.

Adam saw her hand wave from the cab window as the lorry pulled out on to the dual carriageway. Then he started making his way back to Castle Dreich.

CHAPTER 31

BRITISH MUSEUM
(SATURDAY 20TH DECEMBER 2014)

It was five past four when Asa arrived outside the British Museum, still trying to flatten down an eccentric upright piece of hair. 'What's the excitement?' he asked.

Leo, standing behind the girls, stared at the back of Megan's head, breathed in silently through his teeth and shook his head quickly from side to side as if to say *she's gone a bit mad.*

'Leo,' Asa said, 'have you got some sort of twitch?'

Ignoring Leo's red face, Megan ploughed on. 'I've had a message from Adam.'

'Where is he?' said Asa.

Megan explained what she knew.

'Brilliant!' Asa said. 'I always wanted to be involved in this James Bond stuff, saving London, keeping the British end up.' He looked at Rachel, then back at Megan. 'There won't be any *real* danger, will there?'

'There *could* be some danger,' Megan said. 'But hopefully not. All we need to do is go to the nearest tube stations and look for anyone acting suspiciously.'

'Right . . .' Asa said warily.

'Hmmm . . .' added Leo.

'OK – I think,' said Rachel.

'Listen,' Megan continued. 'The man we're worried about is thin, has a birthmark on his face and wears glasses.'

Asa pointed at Leo with a look of sudden and excited discovery.

Megan flashed Asa the sort of look that often precedes violent words or actions. '. . . And he's called Alistair. He might have a large device of some sort for distributing poison gas – it'll probably be really obvious.'

'Maybe he'll be dressed as a London Underground worker and carrying boxes,' suggested Leo.

'Good thinking,' said Megan.

'Or he could trick us by wearing it, like a weird fancy-dress costume,' added Asa.

Megan ignored him. 'There are four possible stations – Adam didn't specify which. So we'll split up, warn each station and keep an eye out. Let's meet back here at five.'

RUSSELL SQUARE

Asa was relieved to think that Russell Square was the least

likely target, as it wasn't on the side of the main British Museum entrance.

He breezed up to a man in a London Underground uniform standing in front of the ticket barrier and the three lifts. 'Hey,' he started, 'how's it going?'

'Can I help you?' The man didn't look easily amused.

'I'm, er, worried that something might be about to happen in this station,' Asa ventured.

The attendant leaned forward until his nose was about six inches away from Asa's. 'Are you delivering a specific threat, son?'

'No, no,' Asa mumbled, backing away. 'I just wanted to check everything was OK and that nobody has carried in any machines . . .'

The man looked as if he was about to speak frankly to Asa and throw him out, but he controlled himself in time. 'We'll be vigilant,' he said bluntly. 'Every part of the station is under surveillance. *You* should remember that.'

'Is it OK if I go into the station?'

'Are *you* a threat?'

'No,' Asa said, 'I just want to get a train.'

'Then you'll *have* to go into the station. The trains are down the lift.'

Asa went down in the lift. It was clear to him that

no one could get a sizeable device past the man at the front and into these lifts, or drag it down the stairs. There weren't even escalators.

He hung around for a while, wandering up and down both platforms until the same man arrived. 'Leave,' was all he said.

GOODGE STREET

Leo strode off to Goodge Street. Megan trusted him to do a thorough job, but was terrified about what would happen if he did discover something. She hoped that there would be police nearby, or at least a tough attendant.

Like Russell Square, Goodge Street was all lifts and no escalators.

Leo headed straight to the platform and did a methodical check. He looked under the seats and examined the tiling, even trying to work out what lay behind locked doors.

Nothing.

An hour later: still nothing.

Leo thought that the whole idea was rather fantastical. He wondered how he would try to deliver poisoned gas. He would have to wear a mask and other protective clothing. He would need lots of the source material, unless it was something tiny and powerful, like the poison those people used in Tokyo. He would need to pump it out. True, moving trains would then disperse it, terrifyingly, through the system, but surely people would see the machine.

Maybe in a tunnel? But the trains ran so close to the wall – they'd squash anyone.

Then one idea led to another and Leo realized exactly how he would do it. They had been really stupid. He had to find Megan.

HOLBORN

Rachel headed off to Holborn Station.

It was large and busy. Rachel wandered up to a young attendant standing by the ticket barrier. 'Excuse me,' she said confidently, 'could you help me out?'

'Of course I can,' he said, smiling. 'What's the problem?'

'I'm trying to find someone – he's slim and . . .' She didn't want to say anything negative. 'And has a sort of birthmark on his face. I think he's lost.'

Agreement being the easiest course of action, the attendant let Rachel into the station without a ticket. But it was soon clear that there was no one matching her description on any of the four platforms, though she looked twice. There was nothing suspicious at all.

Megan wove past people as she approached one of the station's entrances. People were milling around outside the ticket barriers, never still, but not actually seeming to go anywhere. She nudged into several people vaguely matching the description of Alistair, but without noticeable birthmarks.

She was being swept along by a crowd of tourists following a man with a raised umbrella when she saw a slim man heaving a large bag through one of the barriers. A heavy rucksack made him lean backwards slightly. She looked closer but couldn't see his face. He wore a long white cloak. Megan watched him go down the escalator marked *Central Line*.

Megan shouted 'Hey!' half at the man and half at one of the attendants. 'Stop!' Then she saw two police officers leaning over the ticket barrier and laughing with one of the station staff. 'Help!' she shouted. 'Over here!'

The female police officer hurried over.

'There's a man acting suspiciously. Something might be about to happen. He's gone down there.' She pointed.

The policewoman looked surprised. 'What makes you think he's suspicious?' she asked.

Megan was on tiptoe, trying to see if the man was still

visible. 'I'm worried there's going to be an attack. He had a heavy bag and a rucksack. Acting very suspiciously. I can point him out, if we're quick.'

Megan followed the officers down the escalator. As they came to the bottom, just as a train was entering the station, the man was there, halfway along the platform.

'Sir, please stop and stand still,' said the officer.

The man looked around as if someone else was being addressed.

'Excuse me, sir. You! With the bag and the rucksack.'

Fear raced through those nearby. A wide circle formed around the man; some people left the platform, parents shuffling kids in front of them.

An athletic-looking man with a crew cut pounced forward and took hold of the man from behind as Megan and the policewoman arrived. 'Don't try anything,' he growled.

'Why are you doing this?' asked the man with the case. 'I am a good man, a peaceful man.'

Megan was undeterred, though she realized now that he had moles on his face, not a birthmark. Perhaps Abbie had got them mixed up.

The policewoman peered into the man's rucksack. She was cautious, using two fingers and leaning back as if there might be an animal inside waiting to bite her. She only found two large bottles of water and a folded rug. Even more slowly, the suitcase was unzipped – then, all of a sudden, gifts for children spilt out.

'I am a British man, born in London,' he said. 'I know why you stop me; it is not fair.'

Megan looked at the ground, avoiding the man's stare. 'No. You're right. Sorry.' She noticed that the policewoman was also sending her annoyed glances. 'I'm sorry to you as well,' Megan added. 'It's just that . . .' Megan then mentioned that she had a tip-off about an attack.

'If there's a specific threat, we'll have to close the station . . .'

But Megan couldn't be specific, and found it hard to explain why Adam hadn't gone to the police in Scotland. *Usual story for us, the police won't help* was all that he had said. In any case, the police were more concerned to apologize to the man for their own rash behaviour.

After hanging around the station entrance a while longer, and once using her Oyster card to have a quick look round the platforms, Megan went back and waited outside the museum, questions taking root in her mind then sprouting into full-grown doubt. If anything was going to happen, it certainly hadn't yet, and it would probably be impossible to stop if it did.

First Asa arrived, then Rachel. Megan insisted that they went home. She would wait for Leo. So at 6 p.m. they left her.

Leo was out of breath when he finally wheezed up alongside Megan. Before she could tell him about her embarrassing experience, he puffed out a question: 'Which station did Adam mention?'

'Leo, I told you,' she said glumly, 'he didn't say *exactly*.'

'No, no, I know. But what *did* he say?'

'The stop for the British Museum.'

Leo was still out of breath. 'Thought so. He could mean the British Museum station.'

'Yes. But which one?' She was fed up and spitting out the words. She was also worried about Adam.

'It's the name of an actual station, Megan,' Leo said, with a note of victory in his voice, 'but one that closed years ago. It's just up the road.'

'What?'

'Look on my phone . . .' He pulled out his new smartphone and typed in the words *British Museum Station*. Up came pages of entries about a disused stop.

'But that could mean . . .' Megan, won over by Leo's

enthusiasm, looked at the description on the screen. 'That would mean it was—'

'Just round the corner,' Leo concluded as they both started to run.

Excitement dimmed when they turned the corner and found a row of shops where the entrance used to be. Megan asked a man selling flags and other London memorabilia, but he knew nothing of a station; likewise the woman next door selling handbags. After half an hour they both stood on the street looking around in vain, when Leo's phone pinged. 'Oh no,' he moaned. 'My mum has flipped. She's threatening to send out the police to look for me. I'm sorry, Meg. I'm know this is important, and I do want to help, but my mum really would call the police, as you know.'

'You'd best go home. Thanks, Leo, you've been a great help.'

'Let me know if I can help any more later, Meg.' He walked away quickly, glancing fearfully at his phone.

Megan wondered if she had done all she could. She looked at the bus slowing to a halt and checked the time.

Slim, birthmark, glasses. Called Alistair.

A man was crossing the road ahead of her. He was

looking at his watch and had a focused, rather haunted, expression.

Slim, birthmark, glasses . . .

Alistair?

He stopped next to her, just a few feet away, checking that no one was watching. Megan tried to see if she could catch a reflection in her phone, then caught his image in the window of the handbag shop. He went to her left and down a narrow alleyway. Megan turned the corner in time to see him disappearing through a faded and chipped green door.

Alistair went down and down into the old British Museum station.

CHAPTER 32

EDINBURGH
(SATURDAY 20TH DECEMBER 2014)

Abbie sat in the cab, urging the lorry on down the dual carriageway, then round Perth and down the M90 towards Edinburgh, but the speedometer refused to edge over its sixty-two-miles-per-hour limit.

'I can see that you're all het up,' said the driver in his thick accent. 'Is there something I can do?'

'I need to get to my dad as soon as possible,' said Abbie, again frustrated that cars were racing past them. 'He's about to do something really stupid.'

'And where's yer old man?'

'I'm not even exactly sure. South of Edinburgh somewhere – the Glencorse Pumping Station?'

'I remember taking pipes into the place. Bloody great things. And then a turbine. Beast of a job.'

Abbie immediately sat upright, wide-eyed. 'You know where it is?'

'Oh aye.'

Abbie leaned forward. 'You're not actually *going* there?'

'Oh no.' He shook his head. 'Two drops in Musselburgh.'

Abbie sank back slightly. She looked at the notepad on his dashboard and was about to ask for directions.

'But I'll bend the rules an' drop you a wee way down the A702.'

It was late afternoon, and the sunlight was ebbing away. Abbie waved as the lorry swung around and headed back towards Edinburgh, leaving her by the side of the main road in the Pentland Hills, barely a mile from where she wanted to be. The driver had told her trees had been planted to shield the site, which was hidden under a grass-covered roof.

She heard nothing as she walked along the road. No gurgling or whirring noises drifted in on the breeze, just the wintry creaking of oak trees. Then she came to an open gate – unexpected, given the warnings of high security and threats of fines for unauthorized entry. The place seemed deserted. She had expected to have to scale a fence topped with barbed wire, but she walked on to the site unquestioned.

As she turned the corner Abbie saw three vehicles: a couple of Scottish Water Land Rovers and a Toyota Land Cruiser. There was a small brick office to her right. The door was closed, the lights off.

Still no sign of anyone.

The door was locked, so Abbie cupped her hands to the window and tried to look in. She could just about make things out in the gloom. Straight ahead, a noticeboard covered with white sheets of A4 and some posters, and a desk with a computer.

Then with horror, she saw that there were two bodies lying on the floor. Unmoving. Dead.

'They had to be despatched. All wars have innocent casualties. Those who die for our cause will join us on the Golden Planet.' It was her father's voice from close behind her. 'We've been wondering what happened to you. What have you done with Adam?'

Abbie took in a sharp breath. 'I'm not sure where Adam is. He's not with me any more.' Abbie delivered the words she had prepared: 'Dad, I've thought about it and want to see it through with you. That's why I'm no longer with Adam.'

Before he could respond, Abbie's father heard his name called across the small car park. It was Robert, Noah's father, looking pale and troubled. As he strode closer it was Abbie he addressed, though she couldn't tell if his tone was sarcastic or sad: 'You'll be relieved to know that Noah is fine.'

'Who else is here?' Abbie asked numbly, trying to play her part, ignoring Noah's father.

'Oliver.'

Abbie knew he was important to Bolleskine and had brought Adam to Castle Dreich.

Abbie's father immediately gave instructions to Robert. 'Oliver says you have to put on the Scottish Water clothes and stand by the gate. Have you got the weapon?'

'Yes, Mark.' He nodded and uneasily pulled up his coat to reveal a handgun.

Abbie's father gestured for her to go ahead of him towards a metal door in the grassy mound that housed the water-treatment and supply plant. 'Abbie, we're busy doing vital work,' he said. 'You've done a terrible thing by opposing us. But it'll all be over soon and then you'll have forever to prove your loyalty.'

Inside there was a metal walkway leading into what looked and sounded like the engine room of a ship: pipes snaked in all directions above channels of fast-flowing water. She saw a boy, Oliver, opening one of about twenty paint-pot-sized tubs. The drug.

'What's *she* doing here?' Oliver asked with an authority that seemed far beyond his years. 'We don't need any distractions – keep her quiet. This is something we can deal with once we're on the Golden Planet.'

Abbie fought to hide her shock that such words were coming from one so young. 'Dad,' she started, putting her hand on his upper arm. It was one of the few times since this had all started that they had touched.

'Abbie, the world, blinded and smothered by demons, cannot see the truth. We can.' He was like a stranger to Abbie. 'If you want, you can help. If not, you'll have to wait until we're ready to return to the castle.'

'And if you get in the way, you can easily be sent on ahead of us,' Oliver muttered. 'I'm going to get the last two containers.'

Abbie's father was calm, steely. He spoke as he prised open lids. 'Remember, it's not killing. Any one of us who dies today will be taken to the Golden Planet. It is all in the service of the Valdhinians.'

'Do you honestly believe Mum would have wanted this?'

Her father stopped and straightened up, turning to face her. 'That's *exactly* where I have no doubt.'

'She didn't have any time for religion.'

'Abbie, she has told me *herself* that Bolleskine is right.'

'She can't have done – she's dead!' Abbie couldn't stop herself. 'Please, don't be an idiot. Mum's dead, dead, dead!'

Slap.

She recovered from the blow and stood upright again.

'How dare you!' Her father shouted. 'She speaks to me all the time.'

She saw spiders, her dad saw his dead wife. Abbie had always thought that the dark things of our dreams would be fears, like her spiders or Adam's bats. Now she understood that the drug was far more powerful than that.

Gallon after gallon of water was pouring away under their feet, heading for Edinburgh.

Her dad raised his hand again, but this time Abbie caught it. There were tears in her eyes. 'You know the things Mum said, don't you? Remember, Dad, please. *Remember.*'

Mark Hopkins looked down at the drug. 'This is a way for us to be together again. You don't understand.'

'Dad . . .' Abbie didn't have the words to say what she understood about the past and memories and being hard on the outside and soft on the inside. 'Dad, we're too tough to let these people control us. You can be the hero. *Please* listen to me! *Please!*'

The door opened and Oliver stalked in with the last two tubs of the drug, one in either hand. He smiled at Abbie and put them down. 'We're ready to go.'

Abbie's father said, 'Yes, of course.'

Abbie wasn't sure whether he was addressing her or Oliver. Her mind drifted back to being threatened with a gun, then to the rope being passed out of the window at the castle and her betrayal to Bolleskine. She remembered being held underwater. Her father allowing them to pin her down and force drugs into her. She closed her eyes and pushed her lips together, horrified that her father was subservient to a boy.

'If Adam doesn't return, I will lead us on to the Golden Planet,' said Oliver.

Abbie felt she was standing on the edge of a cliff. She ran past Oliver towards the exit.

'Let her go,' said Oliver – perhaps by chance, perhaps on purpose, allowing Abbie the sight of a gun tucked into his trousers. 'We must begin here.'

Abbie ran across the car park towards the main gate, where Robert was watching the road. 'Robert,' she said breathlessly, approaching. 'Oliver says you're to come inside now. He needs you to start the distribution.'

Robert frowned and nodded very slowly. Uncertain.

Abbie moved closer. 'I'm sorry about Noah. He's really friendly. I didn't want to hurt him.' She looked down. 'I was wrong.'

'These are difficult times,' Robert said.

'Can you forgive me?' Abbie held out her palm.

As Robert shook Abbie's hand, she lunged for the gun, grabbing the weapon from his belt and leaping away, then running back to the metal door.

Robert didn't immediately give chase. He was confused and tired – unsure what was right and what was wrong.

Metal stairs creaked.

'What?' Oliver shouted. 'How?'

It was Abbie, gun raised. She had played computer games that involved guns, and holding a real one, looking down the barrel, was terrifyingly similar to the digital version. 'The safety catch is off.' She looked down the barrel, switching the target from Oliver to her father and back again. 'You two are going to move away from those containers . . .'

They stayed where they were.

'Come on – move!' Abbie was nearly at the bottom of the stairs. 'And if anyone does anything stupid, I'm going to pull the trigger. That includes you.' She nodded in the direction of her father.

Robert was coming down the stairs behind her.

'Abbie – this is dangerous,' said her father. 'We're both

armed and I know you wouldn't shoot me.'

'You're wrong. If you do anything stupid, it'll be just like Call of Duty. Bang. Bang.' She glanced down to see how many steps were left. Abbie's hand was steady, but her heart was thumping and her legs shaky.

My own father!

Then – too quickly – Oliver pulled out his gun, aiming it straight at Abbie. Although he was only fourteen, his blue eyes had the determined stare of an adult. 'I want to join my parents. I want to help rule the Golden Planet.' He shrugged a little and gave a low chuckle. 'How about us kids both pull our triggers at the same time? Then the other two can finish the job here.'

Robert was now immediately behind Abbie. Less than a step away. Within reach . . .

But instead he brushed past and went towards Oliver. He spoke hesitantly. 'I'm not sure about this any more. We've come far, but I didn't like what we did to those men earlier. Oliver – why don't you put it down? Abbie doesn't mean any harm. You're just kids.'

Bang.

Abbie flinched.

Oliver had fired a bullet – at point-blank range – into Robert. Then his gun went straight back to Abbie. 'No, I don't think I will put it down. Who is he to speak to me like that?'

Abbie could see out of the corner of her eye that Robert was lying completely still. Some of the blue pipes had red spattered on them. *All of that life, gone. Just bang. The murdering bastard.* She felt a jet of terror inside her, wild like a loose hose, spraying fear and despair.

Abbie's father had pulled out his gun now too. Abbie could see, she was sure, the direction. It was pointing at Oliver. But his eyes were blinking and looking erratically around the room.

Oliver had the wild-eyed enthusiasm of a boy with no questions. 'Go on – pull the trigger. I know where I'm going: to the Golden Planet. All I care is that the drug is put in the water first.'

For a few seconds, while machinery whirred and water bubbled through the pipes, all three pointed their guns, Abbie and her father at Oliver, while he looked carefully down the line of fire towards Abbie's head. He started to smile.

Abbie's father screwed his face up.

Oliver said, 'See you, Abbie, on the Gold—'

Abbie's father pulled his trigger.

THUD.

Oliver, innocent face full of surprise and agony, fell

back into the passing water with a splash, blood seeping into the water supply.

'What have I done?' wailed Abbie's father, seeming drained of energy. 'He was just a kid. What have I done? What have I done?'

Oliver made a thin groaning sound.

Abbie also lowered her gun. 'Come on, Dad. It's all over now. It's finished.' She started to walk towards him.

Her father let out a desperate screech, raising his gun again. 'Don't come any closer,' he panted, the weapon now pointing at Abbie.

'Dad?' Abbie stopped walking and slowly raised her own pistol again. 'Dad, please, I don't want to die. Not yet. Not now.'

Only three paces apart, father faced daughter, both guns now raised.

Suddenly there was the sound of a door being swung open and several sets of footsteps on the metal walkway. 'Police! Stay where you are. Police!'

'Dad, put it down,' whispered Abbie. 'For Mum.' She pointed her gun at her father's shoulder.

Behind Abbie she could hear urgent messages sent and received on police radios. She heard 'one dead' and 'one seriously injured, feared dead', 'ambulance', 'man and a girl' and 'guns' and 'firearms officers'.

'Please lower your weapons,' said a loud voice from the far side of the room.

'Abbie, I was tired. I was confused. Or maybe I was right. There's only one way to find out.' He raised the gun to his own temple. 'If it's true, I'll let you know.'

'Sir, put down the gun down right now and let's talk about this.'

Water gushed behind Mark Hopkins. Violent, erratic, furious water, red with Oliver's blood.

'Sir, put—'

There was a gunshot and Abbie's father fell to the ground.

'Bloody hell!' shouted a policeman into his radio. 'The man has just been shot by the girl.' The policemen ran forward. One grabbed Abbie and the other kicked her father's gun away from where it had spilt. 'We need another ambulance,' the policeman shouted into his radio, pressing the shoulder wound with his other hand. 'The man has just been shot.'

Abbie turned to the policeman next to her. 'Please help him. Please! And get on your radio and send people out to Castle Dreich.' She turned to her father. *Please survive. You're my dad.*

CHAPTER 33

THE FLY GOES TO THE WEB
(SATURDAY 20TH DECEMBER 2014)

Adam stood watching the lorry pull away until it was out of sight.

Then he went into the trees next to the lay-by. He wanted a strategy as definite as Abbie's, ideally one that ended with him at Castle Dreich with a hundred armed police officers – but he had only hopes, not plans.

Getting close to the castle would be difficult, getting inside even harder, and preventing a massacre there *almost* impossible. But doing something was better than being fobbed off by the police *again*.

Despite the overwhelming desire Adam felt to lead an ordinary life, he was drawn to help the other kids left under the castle. He didn't choose to go back – he just felt he *had* to.

Although he had been up since early morning, had travelled through dangerous underwater tunnels and walked three or four miles to the main road, he didn't feel tired at all. Adrenalin drove him on.

Adam headed cross-country towards the loch. He

travelled through the next valley along, which ran roughly parallel to the route to the castle. Adam knew nothing about navigation by sun, but he did understand that it had to stay on his left, and the path seemed to be straight.

Abbie had been right about the geography. Eventually the loch appeared in front of Adam, stretched out like a grey-blue ribbon. *I hope that she can be as clever when trying to talk her father round.*

The loch was shaped like a number 7, with Adam at the very bottom, looking up its length. Halfway along on the left, on a piece of land that jutted out slightly, was Castle Dreich. A path wound its way down the right-hand side along the foot of fairly steep cliffs, and on the left, not as steep but more exposed, were the wide open hills that were above the caves.

It was impossible to get within a mile of the castle without being seen.

If Abbie turned out to have been wrong about one thing, the whole plan would fail. *I'm sure there are boats there*, she had said. *Sometimes I saw people fishing in the distance.*

Adam first saw another little track in front of him, criss-crossed with tyre tracks that made confusing patterns in the thawing snow. *Well done, Abbie*, he half-said. She had been right that a track left the main one to the castle and came down here.

At the edge of the water he saw two small boats tied to a rickety short wooden jetty. One was covered with blue tarpaulin, the other with white. *Excellent.*

Adam looked around him, imagining eyes in the silence – and binoculars peering down the straight line of sight from the distant castle. He crouched down and edged towards the boats.

The white tarpaulin was covered with slush and green mouldy decay. He peeled back the cover and saw a rusty outboard motor and wet brown slats to sit on. The floor was covered in murky water and near the stern he saw cracked boards with mud seeping in from underneath.

He swore.

The other boat was even older. It had no motor and only traditional-looking wooden oars inside. Adam pressed it down into the shallow water and it dipped slightly, but reassuringly bobbed back up. He looked at the castle in the darkening distance; this was going to be hard work.

Darkness comes quickly in the Highlands. Adam hid behind a tree and waited for the night to sweep in like fog. But as the light faded, so did his optimism. His recent life had been spent trying to get away from danger; why was he now trying to return to it?

Megan rescued me.

Abbie rescued me.

I need to rescue others.

He thought of Max and Helen and the others – victims only because they could do something well.

Adam realized that the incoming darkness had almost turned into proper night. He pulled off the rowing boat's cover again, heaved it into deeper water and jumped in.

Although he had rowed a couple of times in an inflatable dinghy on holiday, that experience was not much use when confronted with a more cumbersome wooden boat, which twisted and bobbed while Adam tried to get the oars into position. He had to concentrate hard to make good contact with the water. Fortunately the wind was mild and blowing more or less up the loch in the direction that he wanted to go. His target was clear, despite a gathering mist; most of the lights in the castle were on.

Adam's shoulders and hands, already tired from the climbing earlier, ached by the halfway point, but he became increasingly careful (and able) to dip the oars in quietly and heave to maximum effect. The castle was getting closer, but the mist was turning into a fog, and its lights were becoming more of a dull blur than a clear target. Eventually he could hardly see the building, but he started to hear indistinct voices.

Then a beam of light swung towards him. A ray that felt like it was trying to seek him out. Adam ducked down. But there was no way he could hide the boat. He must be very close to the bank.

Suddenly a voice: 'Who's there?'

Adam made sure that the oars were out of the water, holding his breath as drips of water splashed back into the loch.

On the bank in front of the castle, detailed to security, was one of the six trusted Inner Guard. At this point in the evening, they had to ensure there were no unwanted visitors; as the evening progressed, they would need to be sure there were no unwanted departures.

'Is anyone there?' the man asked again, wondering if he was imagining things in the excitement of the evening.

About to turn away, he saw the front of a boat nose out of the fog. Then the whole craft slowly emerged. It looked empty.

The man stepped into the cold water, pulling out his

radio as the boat rippled into his circle of torchlight. When it nudged against his knee, he could see that it was completely empty: no rower, no oars, almost ghostly.

I need to report this.

Then . . .

A sudden blur followed by searing pain and dazed confusion. The man put his hand to his head. It came away sticky with blood.

And . . .

More pain – on the back of his head this time. He couldn't stop himself falling forward.

Fragments of thoughts:

Grab the boat.

To avoid falling into the water.

Stumbling.

Leaning forward.

Resting on the boat.

Toppling in.

Gently bobbing up and down on the water.

Drifting away.

Sliding into the safe blankets of unconsciousness.

Adam looked at the end of the oar he had used to hit the man. There was no sign that it had been used as a weapon.

He used it to give the boat with the man in it a shove, then sent both oars out into the loch's foggy swirl.

Adam followed the instructions Abbie had given him in the lorry. He picked up a stone that fitted neatly into the palm of his hand and went straight to the castle walls, darting under windows around the back of the castle. *Keep close to the wall and the lights won't get you*, she had instructed. He tried to picture the window that Abbie had told him about: on the side of the castle away from the loch, next to some garage doors. The window led to a small storeroom next to the kitchen.

In the middle distance Adam heard the thin sound of walkie-talkie contact, the splashing of tyres through mud and the low throb of an engine. A 4x4 was approaching the castle. Risking a glance round the corner, he saw headlights swimming in the fog and the incongruous sight of garage doors set into worn castle stone. About ten paces away was the storeroom window. But the whole area was floodlit – and directly in front of the window stood a man. The cult member couldn't have been in a worse place.

Adam put the stone down and pushed his fist into his palm in frustration. There was no way he could smash the window as hoped. And he would be spotted if he tried to dash in through the garage doors behind the car.

Adam slipped to the ground, nose against the castle walls, and poked his eyes round the corner. The garage doors were being opened and the Land Cruiser had stopped.

The driver was saying something out of his window, and the guard disappeared into the garage. Something like, 'Can you park it here, brother?' echoed from within the garage.

Adam sprang up and, sweeping around to avoid the brightest light, took long steps towards the 4 x 4. Finally, dashing forward, he crouched down by the rear number plate.

Silent edgy breaths.

The guard was back at the passenger window. Adam heard '. . . communion . . . departure . . . all together . . . Golden Planet,' and then, '. . . in the boot.'

He stopped breathing. The guard was four paces away.

Adam lay flat on the floor and wriggled under the car. He could see brown shoes plod to the rear of the vehicle, reaching the back the instant that his own shoes disappeared underneath.

The boot opened.

If the car pulled away now . . .

And the boot closed.

The car started to edge forward into the garage. In one second Adam would be exposed, lying flat in the mud in front of the guard.

Rolling over, Adam looked up and saw an exhaust pipe and other tubes and metal rods inches from his head. Just behind his head there was one strip of metal, and it was this that Adam wrapped his hands around – and kept them there, even when the jolt came, and he was dragged through the mud and into the garage.

Finally the car came to a stop and Adam could let his aching arms go. The garage doors closed with a very secure thump. Adam had managed to get back into the building he had escaped from just hours before.

CHAPTER 34

GOING UNDERGROUND
(SATURDAY 20TH DECEMBER 2014)

Although Megan rattled and pushed and shoved against the green door, it held against her strength. She had one or two onlookers, people passing by in their own worlds, but no one seemed interested in challenging her. Megan was too absorbed in her task to think of the people around her or how this must look. She cursed and tried to shoulder-barge the door as she had seen people do in films. But she wasn't powerful enough. She rattled the door again, overwhelmed with frustration.

There was a sudden rush of sound and her shoulders were grabbed. 'Can we help you?'

Megan leaped with sudden terror.

'Asa, stop messing around,' said Rachel. 'We thought it was you, Megan. What on earth are you doing? We were just on our way back from Starbucks and we saw you duck down here.'

'I need to get through this door.' Megan gave it another rattle. 'Asa, are you strong enough to break it open? It's not *especially* sturdy.' Megan gave it an ineffectual kick.

'I could,' Asa said. 'but – y'know – there are laws and things about smashing down doors.'

A small group of tourists shuffled past, trying to find the main road.

'If you don't break down that door, I'll . . . I'll . . .'

Rachel and Asa raised their eyebrows.

'OK, let's do it *together*. Then I'm responsible. And if I'm right –' Megan glared at Asa with a determined eye – 'you can take the credit.'

On the third attempt, the lock cracked open.

Inside wasn't the crumbling, dusty hole that Megan had been expecting. The concrete floor was chipped in places, and the walls were covered in names and other fading graffiti, but it had been swept clean.

'Rach,' said Megan, 'would you get the police? I'm certain that something is going on.' And then to a reluctant Asa, 'You're coming with me.' She walked through the doorway and down the passageway. 'Don't stand there like an idiot. *Come on.*'

Asa shrugged at Rachel. 'My life is one long story of being told what to do by women,' he muttered.

Rachel shook her head and frowned at Megan. 'I can't believe I'm going to get the police so that they can arrest my best friend and my boyfriend.'

273

Asa puffed his chest out. 'Boyfriend, eh?' He strutted peacock-like for two steps. 'OK. Let's go, I *suppose.*'

On the left there was a turn that led to a deep spiral staircase. Frosted plastic covers shielded bulbs strung a few steps apart.

'Come on,' she said quietly. 'Adam has never let me down before.'

The steps creaked and rattled as they descended, and it was only as Megan put one hand on the inner handrail and one on the outer that she appreciated quite how totally unprepared they were. What if the man had a weapon? What if there were others with him?

Asa muttered in a whispery squeak: 'I don't think there's anything down here.' A few steps later: 'Right, we can go back now.'

Megan turned and pointed a rigid finger at him. 'Look,' she pleaded. 'This could be something you'll remember *forever*. If there's nothing, we'll leave right away.'

Asa nodded, tight-lipped. He wanted to say that they should return if there was *something* down this ghostly ghostly staircase.

With a few steps to go, Megan stopped. A noise. Then there was a much louder sound: metal falling on to concrete. And a scraping sound: a something, maybe a bucket, being dragged across a floor.

Megan put the same rigid finger to her lips, then beckoned Asa on.

As they approached the very bottom of the stairs there was a more dramatic rush of noise coming from the right. Rhythmic clangs and jangles accompanied by a draught. A train was passing. Although the station was closed, the line was still in use. But the noise didn't stop entirely when the train had passed. There was another scraping sound. And then a cough.

Asa tapped Megan on the shoulder and pointed upstairs. 'Let's. Go,' he mouthed.

Megan glowered, her jaw and lips tight, but said nothing.

Here the smooth walls had been replaced by damp brick. Arched passageways headed off to left and right, disappearing into darkness. They tiptoed on, until Megan pointed to the right. There was a metal door slightly ajar, bolt and metal clasp hanging loose.

It was clear even from the small section that they could see that something very weird was going on. This room was painted completely black, all six sides including the floor, with minuscule dots of light across every surface. Megan peered inside, careful not to nudge the door. In the middle of the room there was a gold globe, throwing out the specks of light. She nudged Asa. 'I don't like this,' she whispered. 'Let's get help from upstairs.'

But Asa was pointing further down the corridor. There was a man dragging a large container. Asa was open-mouthed with horror. Megan seized his arm and dragged him into the room.

Needle-thin pins of light fired on to them like lasers, criss-crossing the room, confusing, sparkling. There were only two other things in the room: a coat, and a mobile phone on top of it.

Without a second's thought, Megan grabbed the phone and put it in her pocket.

Asa put his head in his hands.

'We're going back upstairs,' whispered Megan, pointing theatrically upward.

Another train was coming, noise gathering in the distance, then loud clattering.

Yes, nodded Asa eagerly as they edged out of the room and silently, despite the other noise, took large steps back to the stairs. They had just turned the corner when they heard a voice.

The man was speaking in a language that neither Asa nor Megan had ever heard – in fact, he was using the made-up language of his imaginary Valdhinians.

After a brief pause, Megan and Asa crept on, back up the stairs.

Then English words, clearer and louder. 'I must be empty of myself. Now is the time. I delay no longer on this evil planet, and with this food will bring others to join us. I must be empty of myself. Others must be empty of themselves. The evildoers must be punished.'

Asa started moving faster. 'Let's get out of here!'

But Megan had turned and was moving towards the voice.

'Meg?' said Asa.

She was beginning to run – *the wrong way.*

'NOW IS THE TIME!' came from down the tunnel, before the words were drowned out by another passing train.

'Meg? Come back!' This time he was loud enough to be heard throughout the tunnels.

Megan ran straight towards the point where the track passed through the disused station. Back down the tunnel, past shapes, words and names sprayed on the walls years earlier, beyond the metal door and two other turnings, before she hurtled out to where the platform used to be, though this was now on the same level as the tracks. The rear carriage of a tube train was rapidly disappearing down the tunnel.

Asa took a very deep breath and followed.

Beside the track there were old sleepers and other discarded pieces of equipment. Turning left, Megan saw these first. Then she looked to the right: immediately next to the wall at the far end of the disused platform there was a man pouring the last of five large containers of a crumbly yellow substance into a metal machine that looked very much like a snow cannon.

The man looked up. 'What?' Mania fell from him, replaced by surprise. 'Who are you? What are you doing here?'

Megan took in the electrical cable running into the tube tunnel, the strange device and the hawk-like, determined man with blank eyes in front of her.

Asa came to a stop behind Megan. His hands were shaking and he chattered in a high-pitched voice. 'We seem to have lost our way.'

Megan shuffled forward a couple of quarter-steps. 'What are *you* doing here?'

The man flicked a switch and the machine started to whirr. 'We shall travel together to the Golden Planet.'

Megan ran towards him. Asa didn't exactly decide to run; it was as if Megan exerted a sort of gravitational pull that dragged him along in her wake. And as she threw herself towards the man, Asa arrived in front of the machine, which was now making a slightly lower growl, beginning to turn the poison into minuscule airborne particles, and stood frowning, trying to work out how to switch it off.

Megan was easily thrown aside, spinning into the mess at the side of the tracks. She didn't have the weight or strength to compete with an adult. 'Just rip the thing apart,' she yelled at Asa.

But Asa only yanked the cord from the side of the machine, and, trailing the electrical wire with him, backed into the train tunnel. He knew he couldn't outrun the man; neither could he flee down the tunnel and risk meeting an oncoming train.

Alistair picked up a metal pole, left years before by a workman, and spoke calmly to Asa. 'Hand that back.' He tapped the pole twice against his leg, then raised it.

'Meg – what do I do now?' screamed Asa. 'I'm *not* enjoying this any more.'

'It's over,' said Meg. She could see that the man was two paces away from hitting Asa over the head with the metal bar. 'Asa – throw down the cable.'

Asa let it fall from his trembling hands.

As Alistair leaned down to pick it up, Megan made her move. She had one chance, so she put everything into it, shoulder first, a barge rather than a push. The man fell between the tracks.

'You're going to have to do better than that,' he sneered.

Megan then shoved him with what she was holding. With all her might. It was only a broken wooden sleeper, not quite half of one, and it nudged the man less than two inches. But once Megan had pushed him those two inches, she fought with all her might to keep him there, pressed against the live rail.

Sparks flew off his metal pole as it rested on the track, and the man writhed in electrified agony.

Megan's piece of wood insulated her from the electricity. Then she understood that the current was holding the man to the rail and she realized the horrific thing she had done.

Pale lights shone on his even paler face. The man was rigid. Dead.

CHAPTER 35

SPIDERS AND FLIES
(SATURDAY 20TH DECEMBER 2014)

Adam dared do nothing more than tilt his head to the left. There was only one person in the car, and he made the sounds that people do when unaware they're being overheard. A sniff, a little cough, jangling of keys. Adam breathed slowly with his mouth open – completely silent.

There was scuffling across the floor and a door opened and closed. Then a *tock* and the garage was dark and silent.

Adam still didn't move. He was unsure what would happen if he just stayed where he was and let events run their course. The kids trapped in the cavern would certainly die. He didn't want that to happen. A lot of stupid cult members would also die. He didn't really want that either. He shuffled from under the car, wincing at his grazed back.

The light came on as soon as he stood up – Adam froze, a second spent working out where to hide – but the garage was empty apart from himself and four cars.

He had no idea what was beyond the inner door. Abbie

had taken it for granted he would get into the storeroom. After a couple of false starts summoning up his courage, Adam eased it open for an instant, just enough to peep through. He saw glimpses of a washing machine and a large chest freezer. A utility room with a tumble dryer, two ironing boards . . . For all the group's lunacy, it still needed the ordinary domestic paraphernalia of a hotel.

He entered and tiptoed forward to another door – and heard voices. He was listening carefully when, without any warning, the door flew open and he had to arch to the right to avoid being hit, narrowly missing a mop and metal bucket. His hand felt for the wooden pole – not that it would be a very useful weapon.

But the person didn't enter the room. Instead they gave an excited message to unseen people: 'Bolleskine is going to talk to us all.'

For a few seconds Adam heard the rustle of movement.

Slowly silence fell, and Adam opened the door on to the corridor outside. He could hear very distant applause and faint laughter, then quiet followed by more applause. They were all listening to Bolleskine.

Adam craned his neck out and peered left and right. He crept towards the kitchen, following Abbie's directions, and put his hand on the door. If there were people on the other side, he would have nowhere to run.

Slowly, creaking and rasping slightly against the floor, the door opened to reveal a large but empty kitchen.

Abbie said that the drug was kept in a large locked cabinet on the left-hand side. He had to break in and either hide it or get rid of it, ideally by washing it down the sink.

To his delight, the cupboards Abbie had told him about were open. But as he leaped forward, he saw, to his dismay, that they were also empty. He put both hands to his mouth to stifle his cry of despair. This had all been for nothing. Perhaps they were using the poison right now.

Then he saw the thirteen jugs. One smell of the peppery liquid inside was enough to tell him what he had discovered. This was the drink that would bring death to the kidnapped children and Bolleskine's followers – the drink that Bolleskine said would take them to the Golden Planet.

Adam couldn't hear it, but at that moment Bolleskine was inviting everyone to drink in honour of the arrival of the Valdhinians. The ceremony would whisk them away to the promised planet. No one was now allowed to leave. Members of the Inner Guard stood at the locked exits. Adam was unsure how many knew they were drinking to their death and how many were being tricked. But they would all die.

Vee and six others were asked to bring up the ceremonial drink – the last drink of this world. Water mixed with the drug and other poisons.

Adam frantically poured the liquid away, but it was only after the first couple of jugs had been emptied that he thought of filling them with clean water.

Eight had been emptied and five filled as Vee started down the stairs to the kitchen.

Thirteen empty. Eight filled.

Then Adam thought of the peppery smell. Collecting a small pot from the other side of the kitchen and skidding across the floor, Adam erratically shook some pepper into the water, blowing away what fell on the work surface, and swilling the liquid with his dirty fingers.

Was there more poison?

Too late –

Excited voices grew louder as they approached the corridor outside the kitchen. Adam was now trapped.

He looked around in panic for somewhere to hide. The windows were too high and too small for him to get through. The door to what looked like a walk-in larder rattled against a lock. There were two fridges full of racks and what little food was left; the oven was a huge device, but not large enough for him; the bin came up to his waist, but one glance inside showed it was nearly full.

Panic sharpening – and then clouding – his frantic mind, Adam was about to grab a knife and try to get into a cupboard when he noticed the dumb waiter. This was a very small lift used to take food up one floor, and it looked just – perhaps – the right size. Dropping the pepper, placing what was already in the dumb waiter – a tray of cutlery – on to the nearest work surface, Adam clambered inside and gently shut the metal door.

Vee and the six others came into the kitchen to collect the jugs. Tangled up in the thrill of the moment, they didn't consider checking the containers, neither did they notice specks of pepper dust on the worktop. Their conversation even masked the metallic squeaking of Adam's hiding place.

Adam ignored the searing pain as he forced his legs against his chest and pressed his head between his knees inside the tiny space. There was silence again.

Upstairs, the followers were neatly assembled in ranks. 'It will not be long before we see the lights of the ship coming to take us to our new home,' said Bolleskine, arms outstretched.

In the kitchen: empty silence.

At the top of the building, in Bolleskine's room, shackled and waiting for their own ceremony with Bolleskine, were twelve chosen children – the most talented of their generation.

Adam was thinking about getting out and trying to inspire some sort of rebellion, when he heard someone approaching.

This time Vee, returning for nothing more than another tray to distribute glasses, spotted the evidence of folded leg visible between the doors of the dumb waiter.

Adam couldn't see her approach – not that there was any possible escape. He only heard the doors snap shut and then a whining sound as he was sent upward. The tiny lift fought to raise Adam's weight, cords and mechanism straining, and eventually delivered him to the floor above.

Adam stayed still, hoping there had been a mistake, but hoping more that he wasn't trapped here, inside such a small space, unable to move. He held in a scream.

But soon the doors snapped open, and Bolleskine was there – relaxed and apparently friendly, as if Adam's extraordinary arrival was the most normal thing in the world. 'It seems that you have arrived just in time,' he said.

In the distance, Adam could see a handful of people queuing up to drink the liquid that he had switched. He was dragged from the small lift and bundled away with a hand over his mouth. He tried to bite and kick and thrash around, but was lifted up and saw walls and ceilings pass.

Then paintings . . .

And finally he saw his own reflection. He had arrived in Bolleskine's mirrored office.

'If only you fully understood . . .' said Bolleskine. 'You are the boy who fulfilled the prophecy. *If he outgrows his thirteenth year, he will destroy Coron and The People.* And you did.'

Adam struggled again as he was forced on to the thirteenth wooden chair and held on either side.

'And it was *one second* after midnight that the prophecy was fulfilled,' Bolleskine continued. 'You are the chosen one. You will lead us on to the Golden Planet.'

One of Adam's hands was cuffed to the chair.

He saw the twelve other children from the cavern. Shackled and exhausted, their fight gone. They looked confused and submissive.

'NO!' shouted Adam. 'If I am to drink my death, it must be done willingly. It has always been said that I must choose my own destiny.' Adam tugged on the one

hand that was chained. 'I command that you release me.'
He glared at Bolleskine. 'I will not run. I came into this
building by choice.'

Slowly Bolleskine nodded at one of the men. A small
key unlocked the metal clasp around Adam's wrist.

Adam sat calmly with his hands behind his back. 'I will
drink first, and if anyone doesn't drink with me . . .' He
looked at the gun that the man on his right was holding.
'Then shoot me.'

'Yes,' said Bolleskine, taking the weapon.

'I won't commit suicide!' It was Max, the young
physicist, hysterical with the desperate terror of death. 'I
won't do it.'

'We must drink,' said Adam, 'or he will use it.'

Bolleskine nodded, laid the gun flat on the table in
front of him, and picked up a silver goblet filled with
liquid. 'You are thirteen: Adam and twelve disciples.
And this is your Last Supper.' With a smile, he raised
the chalice.

Three police cars spun off the dual carriageway down the
muddy track to Castle Dreich.

Two army helicopters from RAF Lossiemouth raced
down the valley towards the castle. News had travelled

288

urgently from Edinburgh and London.

'This is RFR 2-3-K,' said one pilot, reporting back to his base. 'Fog clearing, so we can follow the loch. Over.'

Downstairs, Vee realized that something was wrong. Those who had drunk first had not begun to feel anything. And no one had seen any Valdhinians.

It wasn't supposed to be like this.

She had to find Bolleskine.

Adam raised the small silver cup to his lips. He paused. *Was it the same liquid as he had switched downstairs?*

Bolleskine nudged the gun with his knuckle.

Adam closed his eyes and drank the contents – every drop. He nodded at the other children, silently pleading with them to follow suit. After the chalice was refilled, one by one they accepted the liquid. Then the adults drank. And finally Bolleskine.

Rotors whirred. Lights erratically illuminated the top of the castle.

Fuzzy messages were sent over the helicopter's radio. 'Roger that. We can see the target. Over.'

*

The thunderous buzz of helicopters reverberated around Castle Dreich and spotlights shone in through the windows.

'They're here,' said Adam.

'But . . .' started Bolleskine, leaping to the door that opened on to steps leading to the roof. 'Is that . . . ?' He opened the door and stepped out. Red and white lights swept around the sky. Half excited, half bemused, Bolleskine ascended the steps outside into the cold Scottish air.

Adam's eyes met one of the adult's and they both reached for the gun. Hands slapped on the wooden table. And one person picked up the weapon –

Adam was fastest. He darted away with the gun and ran after Bolleskine.

On the small roof section at the very top of the castle Bolleskine was looking upward, dazzled by the helicopters' spotlights.

'How could you do this?' Adam shouted, climbing the final steps and waving the gun wildly. 'How could you do this to so many people?'

Bolleskine stretched his arms out, opening his chest to Adam. 'Go on, release me.'

Above, men were twisting through the air down ropes, buffeted by the wind.

Adam raised the gun, all the pain of the last year rushing through him and turning into anger.

Bolleskine closed his eyes. Arms wide. Palms open.

And the unfired gun spun away over the castle walls, down and down, until it clattered uselessly against rocks. Adam had thrown it.

Seconds later, police burst in through the main door of the castle.

Bolleskine, eyes still closed, took a step back, and another and another, nearer and nearer to the walls. It was as the first soldier landed on the roof that he reached the narrow strip of battlements that marked the edge. He opened his eyes and stared at Adam in admiration. 'I will see you on the Golden Planet. You again prove that you are the chosen one.' Then he toppled back into the darkness.

Adam sank to his knees. 'No,' he muttered. 'I'm not the chosen one. I'm just a normal kid.'

EPILOGUE

A FEW WEEKS LATER

Adam and Abbie stopped at the bottom of the stairs, facing one another. They were on their way back to the rest of the group. 'I never thought we'd end up here,' she said as a passing policeman smiled at them.

'Thanks,' Adam said, hugging Abbie. 'You were great.'

She held him tightly. 'See you around.'

Megan was walking down the stairs, staring, as Adam stepped away from Abbie. He felt inexplicably guilty and shuffled awkwardly.

Megan avoided eye contact with the departing Abbie. 'I knew that you fancied her,' she hissed, ignoring passers-by in suits.

'Meg!' pleaded Adam through his teeth, catching hold of Megan's shoulders. 'You know that's not true!'

Nearby adults raised their eyebrows.

Megan wriggled. 'How could you?' She turned her face away from him.

Adam pulled her closer and twisted so that he could

kiss her gently. Slowly she raised her head, and started kissing him back.

They didn't hear the others come down the staircase, past the paintings and portraits.

'Megan!'

'Adam!'

They didn't hear their parents.

They didn't hear Asa's hoot or Rachel's slap.

Nor Leo: 'I'm so pleased things are back to normal. Not that I mean that's *normal*. I mean . . . I was just saying . . .'

They didn't see Abbie walk away, off to visit her dad in a nearby hospital.

There were other laughing adult voices.

'Adam Grant and Megan James,' said an amused, commanding, rather upper-class voice nearby. 'Thank you very much for coming to 10 Downing Street.'

Adam and Megan leaped apart, wide-eyed. 'Thank you,' they mumbled together, red-faced with embarrassment. 'Thank you, Prime Minister.'

Across London, in a locked room in a secure establishment, Oliver adjusted his pillow. This was his first day without a drip attached to his arm.

'I'm pleased you're making such good progress,' said

the social worker. 'With your determination, I'm sure you have a bright future ahead of you.'

'I have much to put right,' said Oliver, his innocent blue eyes glinting. 'I'll certainly never make the same mistakes again.'

ABOUT THE AUTHOR

Tom Hoyle is the pseudonym of a London head teacher. Every day he sees first-hand how much competition there is for children's attention: video games, phone apps, films, music . . . , etc. His sole intention in writing both *Thirteen* and *Spiders* was to create 'an action film on the page', with something exciting happening in every chapter.

ACKNOWLEDGEMENTS

With great thanks to TWSG, who commented on every section as it was written, and AW, who again was an inspiring overseer. TAS was a helpful early reader.

Thanks also to Gillie Russell at Aitken Alexander. If it had not been for Gillie, nothing would have reached the printed page.

Macmillan is a wonderful publisher. Thank you to Venetia Gosling and Helen Bray for editorial changes and remarkable tolerance, Talya Baker for copy-editing, Fliss Stevens and Tracey Ridgewell for setting and layout, Konrad Kirkham for production, and Rachel Vale for another striking cover.

I am grateful to all involved in the process who have supported a book written not for them, but primarily for kids.